PUFFIN BOOKS
On the Flip Side

Lucas, her parents, her teacher, her friends – everyone thinks Lettice is barmy. She spends hours staring into her pets' eyes, 'talking' to them, then comes out with ridiculous stories of 'Blobs' and a race of large creatures that no one can see or touch or hear.

But when the animals everywhere begin acting strangely, even menacingly, Lettice's uncanny understanding of animal behaviour and her fears for the future take on a terrifying new importance.

Another gripping off-beat science-fiction story, with a tantalizingly menacing edge, from the author of *Grinny*, *Trillions* and *Robot Revolt*, all published in Puffin.

On the Flip Side

NICHOLAS FISK

PUFFIN BOOKS

Puffin Books, Penguin Books Ltd, Harmondsworth, Middlesex, England
Viking Penguin Inc., 40 West 23rd Street, New York, New York 10010, U.S.A.
Penguin Books Australia Ltd, Ringwood, Victoria, Australia
Penguin Books Canada Ltd, 2801 John Street, Markham, Ontario, Canada L3R 1B4
Penguin Books (N.Z.) Ltd, 182–190 Wairau Road, Auckland 10, New Zealand

First published by Kestrel Books 1983
Published in Puffin Books 1985

Copyright © Nicholas Fisk, 1983
All rights reserved

Made and printed in Great Britain by
Richard Clay (The Chaucer Press) Ltd, Bungay, Suffolk
Filmset in Baskerville

Bunjy

Lucas said, 'Oh, come *on*, Lettice. You did ask for it.' But she just snivelled into her handkerchief and pulled her rabbit, Bunjy, closer to her. 'It's not fair,' she whimpered. 'Not fair.'

Lucas's mouth opened but he closed it. Better not say anything. Better just to think it.

Lettice! What a name for this gangling sister of his! Twelve years old, almost as tall as he was at fourteen, purple-nosed with crying, blue-fingered with the cold – and crying like a child over a Rex rabbit called Bunjy. *Bunjy* . . .

'You'll soak Bunjy, crying like that,' he said, trying to jolly her along. A mistake. 'Oh, poor darling Bunjy!' she moaned. 'Darling, darling Bunjy! Does nobody love poor darling Bunjy, then . . .'

'You can't expect anyone to love poor darling Bunjy when he's not house-trained and makes a mess on the rug in Mother's bedroom,' he pointed out. 'A lambswool rug,' he added.

But of course, Lettice skidded away from this commonsense point. 'Nobody loves Bunjy!' she cried. 'Only me. Only Lettice.'

'Rabbits love Lettice, Lettice loves rabbits,' said Lucas, still feebly trying to be jolly. But still fighting against his inescapable dislike of his sister. He disliked her so much that they seldom quarrelled; quarrelling meant some sort of contact, some sort of closeness.

'Well, I can't help you,' he said at last. 'I don't understand you. You bring the stupid bunny in when you've been told a million times not to; you let it make messes in people's bedrooms; you get yelled at and kicked out; and now you want sympathy. I just don't understand you.'

'Nobody understands, do they, Bunjikins!' she said to the rabbit. 'Nobody understands me but you, nobody understands you but me.'

'Oh, my *gawd*!' said Lucas, and walked away fast, muttering a falsetto '*We* understand each other, don't we, *Bunjikins?*'

Left alone, Lettice wiped her eyes with her hair then held up Bunjy with both hands around his chest. 'We understand each other,' she repeated softly.

She brought the rabbit closer and closer to her face, slowly, until they were eye to eye. At first the rabbit twitched; then it was still.

She looked into its eyes for a long time and said, 'Oh, yes, Bunjy. We understand each other . . .'

'A worry,' thought Mrs Rideout. 'Both of them a worry.' She looked through the kitchen window at her son Lucas, striding along with shoulders humped. He paused to kick the head of a border pink hanging over the path. The flower head snapped off and arced through the air. Mrs Rideout flinched.

Worry. Lucas was a worry. He read and read and read, strange books, scientific books. But not science itself, not proper science, nothing useful, oh no . . . He was going to fail his exams if it went on like this. He was very clever, very clever indeed, they said so at school and in his reports. But he wasn't getting anywhere. All theory, nothing practical. The sort of books he read would never get him through. Science fiction, psychology, genealogy. Never anything practical. Never the things the examiners wanted.

And Lettice. Oh dear, Lettice. Lettice was named after Great Aunt Lettice who was very well off and took a great interest in the children, a *great* interest. One day she would be gone, but all that money would still be there . . .

She picked up a stainless-steel vegetable chopper and began to chop celery very fast. Lettice! A pretty name, certainly, a feminine name, but not the right name for her Lettice, not the right name at all.

What would have been the right name, she wondered, looking across the lawn at her large daughter. Some rather shocking names suggested themselves. 'Really!' said Mrs Rideout sharply, and chopped away at the celery faster than ever.

Lucas went to his father's room.

'Bunjy at it again?' said Mr Rideout, raising one eyebrow at his son. 'A mess in the bedroom this time, wasn't it? Bunjy and your sister Lettice. Oh dear, oh dear, oh dear . . . Don't come in, I don't want you, I'm busy.'

Lucas said, 'I'll come in, then.' He entered the 'study', and his father settled back in his armchair and glowered at him. But Lucas knew he was delighted to be interrupted; if he was careful, he might trap his father into playing a game of chess. Lucas had started playing two years ago but already he beat his father six and a half times out of ten – the scoreboard on the wall showed that.

'Bunjy,' said Mr Rideout, gloomily. 'Bunjy and Lettice . . .' he settled deeper in his chair. 'If I were a proper scientist,' he began, 'instead of a science correspondent – that is, a hack – I would be able to tell you, in scientific terms, what's wrong with your sister.'

'Your daughter,' Lucas said, slyly. His father disregarded him.

'I'd have a name for her condition, a long scientific name,' Mr Rideout said. 'But as things are, I'd just say she's barmy. Nuts. Loony.'

'Slipped her trolley,' Lucas said, in an American accent. 'Blown her stack. Flipped her lid. Can I have a sherry?'

'None left,' his father said, blankly. 'All gone.'

Lucas picked up the bottle and held it to the light. It was half full. 'White man speak with forked tongue,' he said in his Red Indian voice. The two of them were always harking back to the half-century-old radio and TV plays. Mr Rideout had dozens of them on cassettes.

Lucas poured sherry into dusty glasses. They drank silently. Then Lucas said, 'You ought to clean this place up. If you don't, Mother will.'

'Your mother's losing her steam,' said his father. 'She hasn't been round here for months. Still, it could do with a wipe round or something.'

'Fumigation,' Lucas suggested. 'Or a major fire.'

Mr Rideout looked round the room at the piles of manuscripts, the spilling files, the used cups and glasses, the dictating machine rimmed with dirt on the surfaces his fingers didn't touch, the big old IBM typewriter. 'Soon, very soon,' he said, in the high, whispering voice of the High Priest of Infinite Space, 'I must ascend to a higher plane ... What you humans call Death. And then – and then – all this will be yours, my son!'

'Golly gee!' Lucas said wonderingly, taking the role of the Stardust Kid. 'You gotta be kiddin', Pops! All this *mine?*'

'Lettice,' said his father, in his own voice. 'Do you really think she's barmy?'

'I don't know. There's lots of girls like her, mad about ponies and rabbits. Anything with fur on it.'

'One pony, eight rabbits,' Mr Rideout said. 'And that stoat. The one that bit her. Hamsters, dogs, that hedgehog with the eye infection –'

'That's gone, Dad. Dead and buried. You remember, Lettice cried –'

'Don't remind me. I never knew the human body had that much moisture in it.'

'She's a good weeper.'

'Four solid days. And she kept saying that she'd never been able to *talk* to it.'

'Well, that was the eye infection. She can't talk to them if she can't look into their eyes,' Lucas told his father.

'Just what is this business about looking into their eyes? She spends hours at it. Just gazing. I've watched her. It puts me off my stroke.' He waved a hand at the littered desk. Then he said, 'It worries me, it really does worry me. Does it worry you?'

'Everything worries me,' said Lucas, prodding at the dictating machine. He was tired of the subject. '*I* worry me.'

'With reason,' said his father, suddenly angry. 'I wish I knew where the hell you're pointing, Lucas. I don't want you to end up like – like –'

Lucas could have supplied the missing word – 'me!' – but didn't. His half-brilliant, half-successful, half-baked father was the person he loved, the person he could talk to. Yet he despised his father in some ways. He despised himself in just the same ways.

'I don't know,' said Lucas at last. 'I don't understand Lettice at all. I don't think I want to understand her. I don't go for this fur-and-feather thing of hers. It's not my scene.'

'I wish you'd speak English,' said his father, still angry.

But then he too became tired of the subject and said, 'All right. I'll give you a game. Best of three, no more.'

They got out the chessmen. Shadows lengthened in the untidy garden. The room filled with smoke. Downstairs, Mrs Rideout made telephone call after telephone call about a jumble sale.

By the rabbit-hutches, Lettice sat immovable, holding up Catchmouse, the Rideouts' short-haired tabby cat. The faces of the girl and the cat were separated by inches. The cat was almost as still as the girl; only the tip of Catchmouse's tail twitched from time to time.

The air grew colder. The sun was down.

In the study, Mr Rideout moved his queen diagonally right across the board and took a rook. Lucas began softly to whistle between his teeth; his father had him this time. Next the knight, then he'd bring out his rook. Check, check again, mate.

Downstairs, Mrs Rideout, at the telephone, said, 'No, she hasn't telephoned, she said she'd telephone and not a word. I suppose *I'll* just have to phone *her*, it's too bad.' She drank her cup of tea before it got too cold.

By the rabbit hutches, Lettice said, 'It's no good, Catchy, I just don't understand. You can't mean that, you simply can't.' The cat got up, stretched until its whole spine quivered and walked off, tail high, into a currant bush.

'Come back, Catchy!' Lettice called after it. But it was gone, the tip of its tail flicked and disappeared between stalks and leaves.

Lettice shivered, crossed her arms over her chest and slowly walked indoors.

She could not believe the frightening things the cat had said.

*

That evening, the family sat together in the living-room watching television. Catchmouse watched too, unblinking and perfectly content. But then, Catchy watched television even when the set was turned off and there was no picture. If she wanted the set turned on, she sat on top of the set and craned her neck and head over the screen, dabbing at it with her paw.

Old Duff, the Dalmatian, lay with nose between paws. He was not asleep. His experienced old eyes were looking straight ahead at nothing. His breathing was like long sighs. Lettice thought to herself, 'He's remembering,' but dismissed the thought. Duff never said much to her and she couldn't really tell what he was thinking these days.

Duff's eyes closed. He gave a long, wheezing sigh. Sleepy, Lettice thought. The dog's sleepiness made her feel sleepy too. She blinked.

Catchmouse leaped to her feet and stood arched and bristling on the round pink mat with the faded flowers. The cat glared.

Mr Rideout said, 'Ah, here we go again! "Look where it stands! In the same likeness as the king that's dead! Question it, Horatio!"'

Catchmouse leaped sideways, and spat twice.

'Hamlet's father's ghost,' explained Mr Rideout. Nobody listened to him. Everyone watched the cat.

Catchy moved backwards, flinching her head in little twitches, tiptoeing and curvetting, jaws arched and dagger-teeth ready.

'It's the invisible mouse again, isn't it, Catchy?' said Mr Rideout. 'After it, gal!'

'Not a mouse,' Lucas said. 'More like a mastiff.'

'Whatever it is, it's a big one this evening. Isn't it, Catchy?'

'If Duff were a gentleman he'd go and help her,' said Mrs Rideout, smiling at the outstretched dog. Hearing his own name, Duff jerked and snarled and uneasily shambled to his feet, looking about him. His old legs trembled, especially the hind legs. He growled deep in his throat, then walked cautiously towards the vacant space at which Catchy was glaring. He stretched his head forward, still very carefully, and sniffed – shook his head and sniffed again – growled, in a final, 'Don't say I didn't warn you,' sort of way and lay down again where he had been before.

Catchy too seemed to have reached a dead end in her battle with the invisible enemy. Now she tiptoed forward, placing her front paws neatly one in front of the other on the same line. Her head went back and forth, very carefully, as she prodded her nose at whatever it was.

'They all do it,' said Mrs Rideout. 'Cats, I mean. Seeing ghosts or whatever it is. It's funny how they all do it. When I was a little girl, we had a cat called Sooky and she used to do what Catchy's been doing, I can see her now ... Then she gave that up and took to just staring at one particular spot by the corner of the fireplace. She'd stare at it for hours, growling, happy as can be.'

'Dogs do it too,' said Lucas. 'And horses. You know, suddenly rearing up. Baulking at nothing. Rolling their eyes. Throwing their riders.'

Mr Rideout jabbed a finger at the television set and said, 'Do we have to watch this drivel? Because if we do, I'll tell you the ending right away. It wasn't the son that took the car keys, it was the son's mother –'

'Oh, let's see the end of it now,' said Mrs Rideout. 'It's quite good really. Don't you think so, Lettice?'

'I'll just go to my room for half an hour, Mummy,' said Lettice. 'I don't really want to watch it at all.'

As she left the room, Lettice picked up the cat and

tucked it under her arm. Lucas and his father exchanged glances.

'Gone to have a chat with the cat,' Lucas said.

His father shrugged and they watched the end of the play.

The Blob

Lettice lay on her bed with Catchy crouched on her chest. Catchy's breath smelled of milk – Lettice had given her a saucerful on the way upstairs to put the cat in a good temper. Catchy would never talk to Lettice when she was hungry or thinking of hunting or sleepy, hot, cold, twitchy – there were a hundred times when Catchy wouldn't talk. But she was talking now, talking better than she usually did. Lettice stroked the top of Catchy's head and listened.

Or rather, she saw. Their eyes were locked, the girl's sleepy and seldom blinking, the cat's eyes wide and slightly squinting. 'Show me again, Catchy,' said Lettice.

Yet it was quite like talking, too. There were pictures, of course – but also something that could have been a voice, an inner voice, words inside your head. The voice had no tone, no sentences, nothing like that – you just knew you were being told something. First the cat's eyes seemed to grow and grow; the two eyes became one big yellow blur; the pictures formed; the story started . . .

It looked like a sow, Lettice decided, the thing Catchmouse was letting her see. That big black sow she had seen last spring on the farm down the road when – no, concentrate, don't let go, Lettice told herself, it's so easy to let go . . .

A sow. Anyhow, something big, humped, slow. A Blob.

But Lettice couldn't see a face or feet, just a bulk. 'Can't you show me any more, Catchy?'

The Blob wavered. Its shape seemed to be crisscrossed with lines, it wavered and changed shape a little between the lines. Its outlines were vague, always moving a little.

'More, Catchy! Tell me more!'

'Can't.'

'But you must have seen more than that.'

'No more. I saw that.'

Lettice looked again, concentrating hard. There was the rug with the flowers on it. There was the TV set. There was a glimpse of the fireplace. There were her father's feet, not in focus, but there all right.

'Oh, I understand,' said Lettice, feeling frightened. It *was* frightening: the rug wasn't wavering, the flower pattern wasn't crisscrossed with lines – but the Blob, the sow thing, was. Then it did something else – it began to flicker and fade, then reappear. Lettice felt her heart beating.

The cat felt it too: the one yellow eye suddenly became two eyes as Catchmouse moved, annoyed by Lettice's heartbeats. There was no picture any more, only Catchy's mind inside her head saying unpleasant things about her heartbeats. Lettice stroked the cat's head trying to calm it and make it stay. Catchy settled down again and began to purr loudly. The pictures went and all that was left was Catchy saying, 'Very good, oh yes, very good,' because Lettice was stroking her correctly.

'About that thing, Catchy?'

'That's nice, that's the place, stroke me there –'

'No, I want to know about the *thing*. The big thing on the rug. Have you seen it before, Catchy?'

'Yes.'

'Lots of times?'

'Often and often. Sometimes in the other rooms, sometimes in the garden.' This was Catchmouse's message – but it came through as pictures mostly, sudden snapshots of a bedroom, a kitchen, a flowerbed; always with the big Blob somewhere in the picture.

'Did it frighten you, Catchy?'

The question was too difficult for Catchy to answer. Streams of pictures entered Lettice's eyes, a hundred sentences formed in her mind – but none of them made much sense. Lettice kept asking '*Did* it?' to make sure that Catchy wouldn't just shut off, as she so often did. But then she realized that Catchy wanted to tell her, was anxious to communicate. This was unusual.

'You were frightened, weren't you, Catchy?'

Catchy said, 'Yes.' Yet the cat seldom admitted to being frightened, or to any other emotion that made the cat look a loser. Catchy always had to win at everything. Usually, thought Lettice, if you asked Catchy if she were frightened of something – a dog, say – the message you got was full of spittings and claws and furious rage; which meant, 'That dog had better look out, I'll tear him to pieces!' Yet now, Catchy was admitting to being frightened. But then the cat suddenly recollected her dignity and sprang off the bed.

'Oh, Catchy, don't go!' said Lettice. She was wasting her time. Catchmouse was already scratching at the door and mewing. When Lettice let her out, she walked away without a backward glance, tail up and spine slightly arched to make her legs look longer and stiffer.

Lettice lay down again on her bed to think. She could make no sense of Catchy's messages. They were not the messages she was used to. She liked talking to Catchy more than any other animal because Catchmouse was, in Catch-mouse's own eyes, the centre of the whole world – and it was a wonderful world. Catchy was an empress, a goddess, anything you like so long as it is sufficiently grand and glorious. Catchy has drunk a bowl of milk? Loud cheers from the assembled populace! Catchy has stalked a bird? Roars of applause the world over! Catchy feels sleepy? Throughout the universe, lights fade and the stars in the heavens go out!

Thinking of this made Lettice smile, but with affection. After all, Catchmouse was magnificent, from her own point of view or from anyone else's. She did everything well and everything her way.

Lettice thought of the sad little guinea-pigs, their messages full of anxiety; take them out of their cages, they were anxious; put them back, they were anxious. So many of the smaller animals were like that. And the ponies and horses – what fools they could be! They suffered agonies of anxiety, Lettice remembered, most of them centred on people. Would Lettice come and see them or not? When would she come? Why hadn't she come already?

Yet when she did come, even as they told her about their terrible anxiety, they began to forget what they were talking about. They were so easily pleased, so easily diverted. You couldn't, thought Lettice, really talk with horses and ponies. But you could be consoled by them, which was strange considering how anxious they were themselves.

Dogs? Slaves, thought Lettice. Nicer than anyone, nicer than humans, nicer – a million times nicer – than any cat. But slaves all the same. She soon got bored talking with Duff, for instance. Not only because he was old and all his thoughts were really memories; but also because everything he let her know ended with an unspoken question, a request for approval, or permission.

Yet for all this, some of the happiest moments of her life had been spent seeing what dogs saw, feeling what dogs felt, smelling what dogs smelled, running as dogs ran. Even poor old Duff could still take Lettice tearing through the undergrowth, nose down – '*Richness! perfume! stench! Over there – follow it, track it! – over there! Crash and bash through!*'

Yes, Duff could still fill her with loves she never felt of her own accord. The trouble was that these heartfelt loves became sickly and left a taste. '*Fondest mistress, worshipful young mistress – I love you and you love me.*' Followed, of course, by the inevitable anxious question – '*You do, don't you?*'

Unlike cats. Unlike Catchmouse, anyhow – only two other cats had ever consented to talk to her, and they soon got bored with human conversation. Cats didn't care, that was their magic. Cats took what they wanted and walked away. Cats used humans and human possessions and comforts, and gave nothing in return. Cats permitted some people to stroke them, dogs begged anyone to pat them. Cats knew they ruled the world: dogs knew humans ruled it. Cats feared nothing –

She sat up and said, 'No, that's not true. Catchy was afraid of the sow thing, the Blob. She was afraid, really afraid.'

She went downstairs and helped wash up. She did not feel the dishes and cups and saucers and knives and forks as they passed through her hands. She was thinking hard about Blobs.

New York, midsummer

'Hey, lookit!' said Tal. The whole Brooklyn teenage gang, Eddie, Merv, Little Pete and Bronx, stopped what they were doing – throwing nickels into an empty cola can, winner takes all – and looked at the cat.

It was standing in the gutter of the stifling street, bony back arched, scraggy tufts of fur bristling, spitting at the nearside front tyre of a derelict Plymouth convertible. It leapt back, arched again, spat again at nothing. Nothing, or a shadow.

'Some crazy cat,' said Little Pete and threw the can at it. He missed, but only just. The can banged and clattered and rolled. Yet the cat took no notice.

'Like it's spooked,' said Merv, and threw his peaked cap at it. This time it moved, leapt sideways. The gang cheered, the cat ran away, Merv put the can back at the right distance for nickel-throwing.

'All the mogs,' said Bronx, 'All weird, you know? Spooked!'

'So who cares?' said Tal. 'Cats! . . .' As he was the gang's leader, they all decided not to care; and concentrated on throwing nickels into the can.

Warsaw, autumn

The cat was glaring and staring and spitting.

'It's the cold,' said old Mrs Breslaw.

'Don't tell me it's the cold,' said her husband. 'With you, everything's the weather – too hot, too cold, always the weather, the weather always. It's not the cold.'

'Don't tell me it's the Devil!' said Mrs Breslaw. 'With you, it's the Devil, always the Devil.'

'The Devil made witches,' said Mr Breslaw, 'and witches have cats. Who ever heard of a witch with a dog, a rabbit, a sheep? A cat, it is always a cat. The Devil's beast – the cat. That cat has got the Devil in it.'

Mrs Breslaw looked at the cat. It was arched, malignant, wicked, staring at nothing – or was there a blurred shadow? – and hating it. She knew her husband was right, it was the Devil all right, but she would not admit it.

'Witches have *owls*,' she said. 'Don't try to deny it! They have owls also, as well as cats! But you don't see owls doing mad things, bad things. Only cats!'

'*Owls* . . .!' said Mr Breslaw. 'So now it's *owls*! Forget your owls. Look at that cat. That cat has the Devil in it. It's looking at the Devil!'

Mrs Breslaw knew he was right, but said, 'It's the cold. I keep telling you.'

Paris, early winter

'Stop that!' shouted Françine. 'It makes me sick, it makes me giddy! Stop it!' She threw her expensive English cashmere sweater at Minou, but the cat took no notice: it just went on staring, spitting, glaring, each hair erect, all its claws sticking out like thorns.

'Stupid creature!' yelled Françine, bending down to shout in the cat's ear. 'Imbecile! Have you no gratitude for the pretty things I give you? Stop it! Stop it, stop it!' She threw one ear ring then the other at the cat, hurting her ears as she tore them off. But the cat took no notice.

Françine began to cry. Her nerves! All cats were always doing it, always and always, nowadays. The dogs too – that was why she had got rid of Hirondelle, her toy spaniel with the beautiful long ears. He would bark and bark and bark, darting and snapping at something invisible, bark and bark and bark until her poor head could stand no more.

She cried and felt her eye-liner run. In a sudden fury, she kicked Minou with her stockinged foot. The cat jumped sideways, glared at her, then walked fast to the door, tail up. 'Go, then!' cried Françine.

But at the door, the cat paused, turned, poked its head forward to look again at the invisible thing in the middle of the room. 'Go, G O!' shrieked Françine. Through her tears, the middle of the room was indistinct and shadowy.

The glaring cat said, right from the back of its throat, '*Mrrrraow!*'

Françine stopped crying and began to shiver with fear

instead. She would not have minded if that horrid sound had been meant for her, but she knew it was not. It was meant for IT, the invisible thing in the room with her. The thing that, sometimes, she thought she could see as a big, humped, shadowy shape. A Blob.

Animal Crackers

At school, Lettice got into trouble with Miss Langham again.

Miss Langham was the Biology mistress. She was young, pretty, dark, small, straight-backed, crisp-voiced and invariably right about everything. You could imagine her as the perfect secretary – the boss's secretary; as an air hostess, saying, 'Kindly do not panic' as the airliner crashed; as a fashion model even. 'I can't see her as a nun, somehow,' one of Lettice's schoolmates had remarked. 'I mean poor old God . . .!'

Miss Langham was disliked and feared by Lettice: and Lettice annoyed Miss Langham. 'Lettice!' said Miss Langham, 'I don't think you are attending!'

'Oh, I was, I was just looking for my –'

'Lettice, tell me why the larger land animals are necessarily vertebrate,' said Miss Langham.

'Because,' began Lettice. 'Because,' she repeated. Then she changed her mind and plunged to disaster by saying, 'Oh, but Miss Langham, you can have big animals that *aren't* vertebrates. I mean, even apart from crustaceans and molluscs – I mean, you could have a big animal that *isn't* a vertebrate –'

'Name one,' said Miss Langham.

'Well, you probably wouldn't agree with me, but –'

'*Name one*,' said Miss Langham.

'The Blobs,' said Lettice, speaking more or less to herself.

'I beg your pardon, Lettice?' said Miss Langham.

'Blobs,' repeated Lettice, hopelessly.

'Come to the front, Lettice,' said Miss Langham, 'and tell the class about *Blobs*.'

For the next quarter of an hour, Lettice faced the class and told about Blobs. When she faltered, Miss Langham goaded her on again. When she did not falter, Miss Langham interrupted her with questions so that she faltered. It was a good quarter of an hour for the class and perhaps for Miss Langham, and a very bad one for Lettice.

Yet Lettice did not break down. Indeed, as her hopeless recital staggered on, something unusual happened to her. She felt, growing inside her, a determined lump of considered dislike for Miss Langham and what she represented. So instead of collapsing into dampness and snuffles, Lettice actually hardened herself through the whole endless quarter of an hour.

At the end of it, Miss Langham had drawn out of Lettice the whole story of the Blobs (giggles from the class!) – the talks with Catchy (smothered laughter!) – and Lettice's belief in a race of large animals that nobody could see properly, or touch, or hear . . . and this race had something to do with all the stories about odd animal behaviour (outright laughter!).

So Lettice made a fool of herself. Yet, for perhaps the first time in her life, she somehow managed to keep tatters of dignity about her. She had not given in, or shifted her ground, or let Miss Langham walk all over her. Indeed, the last word was Lettice's. Miss Langham, now made prettier than ever by an angry brilliance in her eyes and a flush of colour on her well-placed cheekbones, said, 'I think that is all, Lettice. You may return to your place.' And Lettice, walking back to her desk, said – quite steadily and without her voice going funny – 'It may be enough, Miss Langham, but it isn't all. It's only just started.' The class did not snigger.

When the bell rang, Miss Langham said, 'Please stay behind, Lettice.' So Lettice did.

'Lettice, your work is unsatisfactory. You are sloppy in everything you do. And now your behaviour is becoming ridiculous.'

'I only did what you told me,' said Lettice.

'You wasted a lot of class time with your absurd –'

'You *made* me do it, you *told* me to stand in front and tell them –'

'Lettice, I'm warning you! –'

Then they both paused, having got nowhere. The pause lengthened. At last Miss Langham said, 'Lettice, you can't be as stupid as you pretend. You put yourself in these ridiculous positions – making up this story about invisible animals – saying you can talk with animals –'

'They're *not* invisible. Just very hard to see. And ordinary animals can see them all right.'

'You don't really believe any of the things you have been saying, Lettice?'

'Of course I do. It's all true, I wasn't just making things up.'

Another pause.

Miss Langham said, 'Lettice, you are rather a – a strange girl. I cannot pretend that I like you very much or approve of you, but, then, I don't have to. I am simply one of your teachers. Liking and approval need have little to do with our relationship.'

'Either way,' Lettice interrupted defiantly. She was surprised by her own bravery.

'Either way,' said Miss Langham, raising one eyebrow. 'But I won't put up with too much nonsense from you, Lettice, because I mustn't. Being a teacher means more than just teaching.'

'Form our characters,' mumbled Lettice.

'Quite right,' said Miss Langham. 'I'm supposed to form your characters, which may sound very old-fashioned and unlikely to you, but never mind that. My character and yours are very different. I am a vertebrate creature; I have a backbone, which no doubt you despise. You seem to be one of the Blobs you described – things without backbones. Invertebrates. And you don't want to change, do you? So what do you think I should do, Lettice?'

'You can do anything you like!' said Lettice, coming to the boil. 'Lots of punishments you could give me . . . A bad report, anything you like!'

'I could, but I won't,' said Miss Langham. 'Listen, Lettice. You insist that your Blobs – your strange animals – really exist, don't you?'

'Yes, I do. I do.'

'Then your "punishment", if it is a punishment, is going to be this. You are going to produce a properly documented statement of the things you were talking about in class just now. You are to persuade me, by any means you choose, that you are right; that animal behaviour has changed, that there is real evidence for your Blobs. But no sloppiness, Lettice, I want the job done properly and tidily and completely. And *cleanly*, Lettice. None of your usual finger-marks and stains and messiness.'

'All right.'

Miss Langham looked closely at Lettice's downturned face, trying to make herself feel some sympathy and warmth for the girl. She made her voice lower and softer when she said, 'You are very fond of animals, aren't you, Lettice?'

'Yes. And I know a lot about them. Probably more than you in some ways.'

'You insist that you can talk to them?'

'Yes. I can. I do.'

'All right, Lettice. We'll leave it at that . . .'

As it turned out, Miss Langham was punished more than Lettice. Miss Langham worried, for days after, about her treatment of Lettice and her attitude towards a girl she could not like.

Lettice, however, had no need to worry. She had always disliked Miss Langham; she continued to dislike her; but she did not think about her. For, largely due to Miss Langham, she had more interesting things to think about.

That very evening, Lucas threw the newspaper over to Lettice and said, 'There's a story for your pongy old scrapbook. Animal crackers or whatever you call it. Down at the bottom of page eight. Your furry friends seem to be going ape.'

She found the paragraph. It was a small one headed

SHEEP DIPPY?

A flock of two hundred sheep
turned on Mr John Haslett, farmer,
of Corfe, Dorset and pinned
him against a stone wall for
two hours. Mr Haslett attributes
the incident to chemicals in a new
sheep dip. Mr Haslett was unhurt,
'But my dinner was cold,' he
complained.

Lettice said, 'I read that yesterday, in the evening paper.' She did not tell her brother that she had already assembled a pile of such clippings. Later, lolling on her bed, she opened her scrapbook and re-read them.

'KILLER DOG PACK ROAMS STOCKBROKER BELT' . . . Residents of Leatherhead and Dorking, she read, were being kept awake at dusk by the howling of between fifty and a hundred dogs, hunting in a great pack. The story did not tell what they were hunting.

'SO THE VET CALLED THE DOCTOR!' A very short story about a vet who one evening attended a little girl's sick pony and was attacked by other ponies. A doctor had to be called to treat the vet, who was kicked.

'WIDOW'S MERCY BID FAILS – ROVER MUST DIE.' An eighty-year-old widow's little mongrel dog turned savage and bit her. This story had not interested Lettice because the dog was very old and old dogs can turn 'funny'. It interested her now, however, because of a paragraph she had not really bothered to read before:

> 'He'd just stand and stare and sort of tremble,' said Mrs Henning. 'It happened every evening. Well, I got sick of it, you know, so I said "Come on, Rover! Talk to Mother!" and he wouldn't listen, so one evening I just patted him and then he went quite distracted, he'd got his teeth in my wrist and nothing I could do would make him let go. And now he's got to be put down,' she added tearfully.

'Every evening,' thought Lettice. 'Every *evening* . . .'

She flicked through the other cuttings. 'THE INVISIBLE MAN?' Story about a dog that stared at nothing for two days.

Similar stories headed 'CAT-ATONIC TRANCE!' . . . 'COME OUT, COME OUT, WHATEVER YOU ARE' . . . 'DO PETS SEE GHOSTS?' . . . 'SEEING THINGS!' . . . 'HOW CRUEL CAN WE GET?' (family abandons dog on motorway 'because it would keep staring').

None of the stories was given much space. The widow's

story was the longest but not because of the dog's behaviour; it was the 'human interest' that mattered to the journalist, the poor old lady who had to say goodbye to her dog.

She read through the stories again. 'Evening,' she murmured. '"Later that evening ..." "The family was watching TV when ..." Always in the evening!'

Duff shuffled into the room and rested his chin on the edge of the counterpane, looking soulful. He wanted to be allowed to come on the bed with her. 'Oh no you don't!' said Lettice, then changed her mind.

'All right, Duff,' she said. 'You can come up. But only if you talk. You understand, Duff? Talk.'

The dog clumsily jumped up, tail wagging, and turned round three times on the bedclothes, making itself a hollow. But Lettice took hold of his front legs and pulled him towards her until girl and dog were eye to eye. 'Come on, Duff,' she said. 'Come on, come on, tell me things.'

Duff's Story

'You like me, don't you?' Duff said – but there were no words, of course, just pictures in the amber-brown eyes, and a knowing between them.

'You do like me, don't you?' he insisted. 'Because I love you, I'd do anything for you, anything at all –'

'Tell me about the things you see, then.'

'Oh, yes, anything at all, I'd do anything you asked me. What was it you asked me?'

'Tell me about the things you've been seeing.'

'I saw a new mess in the garden, another dog has been here, a strange dog –'

'I don't mean that sort of thing. *New* things.'

'It was a new mess. A new dog. I don't know that dog.'

Lettice shook Duff gently. 'Listen, Duff, stop being a silly old thing, tell me about the new thing you don't like, the thing you bark at, the thing that makes Catchmouse frightened.'

'No one must be in our garden but us.'

She shook him again as if to shake new patterns into him. Duff's mind was like a kaleidoscope, lots of brightly coloured, meaningless things forming patterns that jogged and scattered. 'In the house, Duff,' she said. 'Is there something new in the house? Something you don't like?'

'I do like talking with you,' said Duff. 'You are my friend. My best friend. My dearest, closest friend. Please, if you don't mind, stop squeezing my front legs.'

'Something new in the house, Duff. Tell me about it.'

'Oh, that's not new, the thing I bark at. It's the same old thing.'

'*What* thing?'

Duff rolled his eyes, trying to think, and said, 'Oh, you know. It. *It*. I T. *That* thing, the thing I bark at.'

'Describe it to me, then.'

'I can't, it's changed, it's not the same as it always was.'

'But you said it's the same old thing.'

'Oh yes, it hasn't changed. Yet it's different. But it's I T all right.'

Lettice said, 'Tell – me – about – I T.' She accompanied each word with a little shake of his legs.

'Which one? There's more than one.'

'All of them.'

'But they're all the same It.'

'Then tell me about them.'

'Well, they're always there, aren't they? Blobby.'

'Concentrate. *Show* me.'

He made a picture. She saw piano legs. They went out of focus. At first she thought it was Duff's fault, but then she realized that the blobby blur was right. It was what Duff meant her to see. It was Catchmouse's sow thing.

The picture jerked, faded and was gone. 'That's what It's like,' said Duff, pleased with himself.

'Show me some more, Duff. More of them. Show me how they're changing.'

'They're different, they're getting clearer.'

'Clearer? Show me!'

Duff tried, but Lettice saw no clear pictures. 'You couldn't see them at all before, they just made a haze like heat,' the dog explained. 'But now It – they – are clearer. But I can't remember properly . . . Oh, and now I can smell them!'

'What sort of smell?' Lettice demanded.

'They smell . . . wrong, so I bark. I often bark,' he said, virtuously.

'All right, Duff, you're being very good. They're getting clearer –'

'Darker. And they flicker. And they smell worse.'

'What do they smell like?'

'Foreign.'

'What do you mean? Foreign like the new dog in our garden?'

'No, foreign. I told you, foreign.'

He was getting impatient with her, Lettice realized. She understood why. To a dog, smells were everything. The language of smells was the one language Duff spoke instantly, fluently and comprehensively. He couldn't understand her lack of education about smells, any more than she could tolerate his slowness in putting thoughts together, or keeping to the point.

'Please explain "foreign",' she said humbly.

'"Foreign" means – it means – it means *not us*. Not dogs, cats, fires, carpets, cars, you – not anything. It means something from somewhere else, not a proper thing.'

'A thing you can't lick or bite?'

'Yes, I suppose so, I suppose that's it. Let me tell you about the new dog that was in our garden –'

'Is the smell of the new dog "foreign"?'

'No of course not, it's a dog. Dogs are us.' He tried to get up and move away, but she held him and said, 'Duff! Duff! Down, Duff!' He gave in, unwillingly, with a soft, annoyed woof.

'What else is foreign, Duff?'

'Nothing else. Only the blobby things. Oh, the noise boxes are a bit foreign, they smell foreign, but at least you can see they're there.'

'Ah,' said Lettice. She let him go because she wanted to think for a moment. Anyhow, he was tired by now, his mind and his legs were twitching.

She understood what he meant by 'noise boxes': she had glimpsed the television set, the radio. He often described things he did not understand as 'boxes'. There was the howl-box (vacuum cleaner), blankbox (ancient washing-machine rusting away under the house), foodbox (the fridge), badbox (telephone – Duff feared it because people talked at it to something invisible).

But the box he had shown her was the television . . .

Evenings, she thought. Always, things happened in the evening.

It was in the evenings that people watched television. It was in the evenings that the animals began behaving in their strange new way. The sheep ganging up on the farmer, Duff's outburst, the widow's dog biting her, Catchmouse's glaring and staring – always in the evenings. Always at television time.

She had relaxed her hold on Duff's legs. He looked at her sideways, cunningly, and sneaked out of the room.

Kalabza

Miss Langham said, 'Very well, Lettice. Let me see your work.'

Lettice handed over the file. It was two inches thick and solid with her own writings, newspaper clippings and pages cut from magazines. Miss Langham managed to keep her expression unchanged. She might at least have raised an eyebrow, thought Lettice.

Miss Langham began reading, turning over sheet after sheet with her taper-nailed, pretty fingers. Lettice admired her eyebrows, which formed two perfectly equal brush strokes, level and elegant. Her lashes were long, her hair had that springing liveliness from the parting that spoke of vigorous health, perfect cleanliness. Lettice tried not to think of a big, fat custard pie – a custard pie, with plenty of frothy eggwhite on top – jammed right on top of Miss Langham's lovely, healthy head.

Miss Langham said, 'When did you begin compiling all this material, Lettice?'

'I was thinking about it before we had – before –'

'Before our row. But you did not begin cutting out the pieces from the paper until two weeks ago, is that right?'

'Yes. When you told me to.'

'There are a great number of cuttings.'

'I told you there would be. I told you that the animals were behaving funnily –'

'Yes, I remember you saying so.'

She continued unhurriedly to turn the pages. She read Lettice's own handwritten pages with care. At last she said, 'You have done a very thorough job, very neatly. I congratulate you, Lettice.'

Lettice wanted to say, 'Is that all?' but said nothing.

Miss Langham bent down to pick up her own briefcase. She opened it and produced a file not unlike Lettice's. She turned the pages to a cutting identical to one of Lettice's and looked up. 'Snap!' said Miss Langham, and smiled. Her smile was unexpectedly charming.

'What do you think about it all, Miss Langham?'

'I think I was wrong and you are quite obviously right.'

Lettice, amazed, said, 'But that day, when you made me stand up in front of everyone –'

'That day, I thought you were wrong and I hoped I was right.'

'Hoped?'

'Oh, I don't mean "hoped" about the animals . . . I mean, I hoped I was doing the right thing as your teacher. Discipline and character and all that sort of thing . . .' She stopped for a moment, embarrassed, and said, 'I'm not all that much older than you girls, you know. It can be very difficult sometimes, particularly with –'

'With people like me? Untidy people?'

Again Miss Langham smiled. 'Yes, that's just what I mean. People who make me nervous; people like you, Lettice.'

'Nervous! *I* make *you* nervous?'

'Yes. Because I can feel your dislike for me. Because we are so very different. If I were not your teacher, it would not matter. But I am, so we are bound to be – enemies, in a way.'

Lettice thought about this and found it to be true. Had Miss Langham been merely a neighbour, she would have been just Miss Langham. Miss Langham, teacher, was something else.

'That day in class,' Miss Langham continued, 'I thought you were being stupid, untidy-minded, fey, whatever word you like. But you've proved your point. You've proved yourself right. So now, I hope, we needn't be enemies. Perhaps we can become colleagues?'

'Colleagues,' said Lettice. The idea was not unattractive. 'Colleagues in what?' she said. 'I mean, we're both agreed now that something's happening with the animals, here and in lots of other places. But we don't agree about the Blobs, the Its – the things you made me tell you about in class.'

'Don't we?' said Miss Langham.

'But of course we don't. You remember in class –'

'It's like ghosts and spiritualists and all that sort of thing as far as I'm concerned,' said Miss Langham. 'I didn't believe you when you said that you could talk to the animals that day: I don't *believe* you, not properly, now: but I don't *disbelieve* you any more. Look, we've got to be frank with each other. That day, I thought you were just playing an act of the sort I particularly dislike. Now I think differently. It wasn't an act, I know that now. But nor is what you say necessarily the truth.'

'I know. I quite see that, I didn't expect you to believe me –'

Miss Langham had been fiddling with her handbag, not listening to Lettice. Now she said, suddenly, 'Do you know of a man called Zafar Kalabza, Lettice? Doctor Kalabza?'

'Doctor Kalabza! Of course! I mean, he's always on TV. Showing off, waving his arms about. Those science programmes –'

'Yes, those science programmes,' said Miss Langham, pursing her lips with distaste. 'Those awful programmes . . .'

'I don't actually know him, of course,' Lettice said.

'I do,' said Miss Langham. 'I once knew him rather well.'
She sounded almost guilty.

'Is he as phoney as he looks?' asked Lettice. 'The way he
dresses and everything . . .'

'He is even *phonier* than he looks,' Miss Langham said.
'And what is worse, Lettice – he is not phoney at all!'

'What do you mean?'

'I honestly believe him to be a genius. Did you know he
won the Nobel Prize, Lettice? The highest international
award a scientist can gain?'

'Oh, that. He never lets you forget it,' Lettice said. 'Always
drags it in somehow, on TV.' She paused and said, 'What
about him, Miss Langham? Why did you ask me if I knew of
him?'

'Because,' Miss Langham said – and now she looked guilty,
even furtive – 'Because he knows of *you*, Lettice. I've told him
about you. You and your interest in animal behaviour. And
communication with animals.'

Lettice stared at Miss Langham, too confused and angry to
speak.

'I didn't mean to do it,' Miss Langham said, hastily. 'It
just – *happened*. You see, we correspond – I was once one of his
students and he insists on writing to me, and – oh dear, he has
such energy, he is so persistent, Lettice, once he gets an idea
in his head he won't let go –'

'Why did you mention *me*?' Lettice said, coldly and
angrily.

'Because he's like you, he's deeply interested in the strange
ways animals have been behaving recently . . . and talking to
animals . . . I'm afraid I let slip the things you said. And he
pounced on everything and telephoned and kept writing me
letters –'

'What letters?' Lettice said, stonily. 'What have they to do
with me?'

'Oh dear, I suppose it would be best if I showed them to you,' said Miss Langham. She opened her handbag and produced a bundle of airmail letters. Her hand shook. The letters spilled.

Lettice bent down to pick them up. One of them had fallen open and Lettice could hardly avoid reading the big, clear handwriting. The letter began, 'Charmingly Curvilinear and Utterly Desirable Schoolmarm, object of my Forbidden Fantasies –'

Miss Langham blushed as she took this letter. 'His prose style is rather lurid,' she said faintly.

'What does he say about *me*?' Lettice said.

Miss Langham recovered rapidly. Her blush faded and her hand was steady. 'Read the letter,' she said. 'Read it aloud.'

Lettice read it. 'It begins, "My adorable . . ." Oh, I'll skip that. It goes on in French, I'm not much good at French –'

'How fortunate,' said Miss Langham, tightly. 'Read the second paragraph. The typewritten part.'

Lettice obeyed. '"Dr Kalabza's dictation,"' she read. '"Regrets unable continue personally, packing for New York Nobel Convention. Says, very interested in the girl Lettice. Does not consider the girl's claims unreasonable. Many reports of human–animal communication throughout history. Dr K. has personally conducted encephalograph tests to attempt to establish reality of such communications" – What does that mean, Miss Langham?'

'An encephalograph is a machine that records brain patterns. If a human could indeed communicate with animals, the encephalograph readings would echo each other in some way.'

'You mean he does horrible experiments on poor animals?'

'I mean nothing of the sort. There is nothing horrible about taking such readings. Do go on with his letter.'

Lettice bit her lip and read on. '"Dr K. will send results of his own and other researches using dogs, horses, cats, dolphins. The most recent experiments are the most interesting and promising, he says; latest equipment producing extraordinary results. He has no doubt that such communication is and always has been possible: but today, meaningful communication may soon be shown and proved.

'"Dr K. now making a joke about breathing up nose and will follow you anywhere. Point of joke not clear.

'"Dr K. says, your girl particularly interesting because she says she *sees* images or pictures in animals' minds. She receives real information, not just emotional messages. This claim most unusual and must repeat must be investigated.

'"Dr K. says, do not dismiss girl's theories about recent examples of odd animal behaviour. He says, odd behaviour documented worldwide, the girl is right and you are wrong. He says you are adorable when wrong.

'"Dr K. getting very excited (you know him) and says coming to Europe soon, must repeat must meet the girl Lettice, perhaps she holds the key to –"

'Now the letter finishes in his own handwriting,' Lettice said. She glimpsed a large, untidy row of hearts and kisses and a huge, sprawling signature, ZAFAR.

'He sounds a bit . . .' said Lettice.

'He is a bit . . . whatever you were thinking,' Miss Langham replied. She was looking rather pink again. 'It doesn't mean anything, of course. He's a sort of – sort of box of fireworks . . . Always exploding and whizzing about and getting wildly excited. But the thing is, Lettice, that he *does* things. He doesn't just appear brilliant, he is brilliant. He *achieves*. When you meet him –'

'Meet him?' Lettice said. 'I'm not going to meet him! Ever!'

'He says he must, repeat must, meet you,' Miss Langham reminded her.

'He can say what he likes! I won't meet him!'

'You won't?' said Miss Langham. She raised one eyebrow and put the letters neatly back in her bag. 'Hmmm,' she said.

A day later, Lucas visited his father's den.

'Chess?' Lucas said, persuasively nudging the board towards his father across the cluttered table in the study.

'No. Shut up for a moment. I want to hear this. You should hear it too.' Mr Rideout fiddled impatiently with the radio. One side of the room was filled with ancient electronic gear. There were tape-recorders, relics filled with relics – he was always listening to terrible old radio plays, half a century out of date. There was the radio he had made himself from junked transistor sets. A mess, this radio. But it gave him what he wanted. It brought in Russia, America, Rome, broadcasts from anywhere.

'Got it!' he said, contentedly, as voices suddenly cleared and filled the room. 'New York! Listen, Lucas . . . The Nobel Convention. Should be worth hearing. They're bound to talk about animal behaviour.'

'Oh, *that*,' Lucas said, without interest. He'd seen and heard enough about the strange behaviour of animals. The dogs and cats and horses and pigs and rats and mice were going mad. So what? Still, his father was a science correspondent and had to be interested. Lucas lay back in the shabby armchair – it reeked of Duff – and half-listened to what the world's scientists were saying.

The bored, grating, American voice that translated the words of a Russian scientist said, 'He's saying, the agenda is being departed from. He objects to that. He says they should be discussing the wheat rust, not these general matters. He objects to that. He says they should be discussing Russian scientists' work on symbiotic parasites of grain crops. He says, he objects to –'

Lucas said, 'Dad, are you really listening to all this? Wouldn't you rather play chess?'

'Shut up,' his father muttered, fiercely; and leaned closer to the speakers. Lucas knew why. For suddenly it was Doctor Kalabza speaking, cutting across the Russian's words, ruthlessly interrupting the dreary blur. It was unmistakably Dr Kalabza's voice: piercing, high-pitched, cutting, vainglorious, speaking too-perfect English.

'Oh, cannot we talk of something *interesting*?' Doctor Kalabza's voice said, very loudly. 'Must it always be our Russian friends, and their so unfortunate problems with wheat? Russian *corn*, always Russian *corn* . . .' The 'corn' was an insult.

The radio speakers brought the sound of muffled uproar. Mr Rideout grinned. Lucas rubbed his hands together and sat forward.

The American voice, very close to the microphone, said, 'The Russian party is saying that they object. Now three of the Russians are standing on their chairs waving order papers. Doctor Kalabza is smiling at the Russians and waving right back at them. The Russians are objecting some more. Doctor Kalabza is smiling some more. Now Doctor Kalabza seems to be conducting an orchestra, he's kind of conducting the Russian choir –'

The harsh, flat American voice suddenly broke up. Its owner was laughing. So were Mr Rideout and Lucas.

'*Animals!*' cried Doctor Kalabza, loudly and clearly. 'Farmyard animals! Oh, not *you*, my dear colleagues! – do not mistake me. I was merely suggesting a better subject for consideration. The behaviour of animals – the dogs and cats, the other animals, the way they are behaving – surely that is the most important and absorbing matter for us to consider? Such extraordinary changes, dear friends, such extraordinary reports from every quarter of the globe! Think what has happened!

'Always, until now, man has told the animals what to do and always has been more or less obeyed. Man has said to the pig, "Be a long-backed pig with more bacon" – and the pig has obeyed. To the greenfly, man has said, "Die when I spray you" and the greenfly has obediently expired. To the horse, man has said, "Have great muscles for hauling" or, "Be slender and long-muscled for the racing!" and the horse has obeyed. Sometimes Nature has revolted and said, "No, my greenfly shall become used to your sprays!" or, "My rats shall resist your poisons!"; but even then, man has understood his own mistakes . . .

'But now – so suddenly! – so mysteriously! – the animals have decided to say, "NO!". And this presents us with a problem, a very great problem. What if the gentle cow refuses to give us our milk? What if the lamb refuses to go to the slaughter? What –'

'What about the Doctor telling us of a cure instead of describing the disease?' interrupted an English voice, good-naturedly.

'Communication,' replied Doctor Kalabza, instantly. 'We must ask the animals what they are doing and why.'

'And how does the Doctor intend to do that?' said the English voice. 'Can he *talk* to the animals?'

'Alas, no. I cannot do that. *But – but*, my friends! – I think I know of someone who can!'

And then the Russians were shouting and the President was hammering for order and there was nothing left worth listening to. Mr Rideout switched off.

Lucas said, 'Who is he? That Doctor Kalabza?'

'Anyone who's ever watched TV knows who he is, so you know who he is. You never stop watching TV, you're glued to the goggle-box –'

'No, I mean, who is he *really*? All the box shows you is a sort of show-off superstar person . . .' Lucas could see this person in his mind: vaguely Indian looking, but not dark – yet with waving, glossy black hair, worn quite long, and with Indian-looking eyes that flashed. He could see the neat, slim body, the flourish of the narrow hands, the endless movements of the mouth (Doctor Kalabza never stopped talking), the teeth like a toothpaste ad. . . . He could see all this, yet had no idea of the real man, the man beneath the public man.

His father told Lucas, 'He's a superstar raver who also happens to be a first-rater. Someone who is deservedly pre-eminent in his field.'

'Zafar Kalabza . . .' Lucas said. 'Sounds more like a stage magician. Is it his real name, do you think?'

'Of course not. He was probably born Sid Sausage or Fred Fryingpan.'

'Is he an Indian, or what?'

'I've no idea. And it wouldn't be much use asking *him*.'

'You mean, he's a liar?'

'No, he simply avoids inconvenient truths. Even in his science. Once he's got an idea in his head, he simply bangs away at it. That's how he made his extraordinary discoveries about amino acids and genetic –'

'You mean, everyone else thought he was wrong? But he was right?'

'Astoundingly right. He changed the whole course of – Look, why this sudden interest in Doctor Kalabza?'

'Well, obviously, because of Lettice.'

'*Lettice?*'

'He said something just now about communication . . . knowing someone who can talk to animals. Wouldn't it be funny if he meant Lettice?'

Mr Rideout regarded his son with wide-open eyes and shook his head slowly from side to side. 'What an incredibly stupid boy you are!' he said at last.

'I can still beat you at chess,' Lucas said. And he did.

Violence

While Lucas talked to his father, Danny Matheson scowled and felt lonely.

Danny Matheson was ten years old. His interests were playing soccer, watching soccer on television, going to soccer matches and talking soccer. In summer, when there was no soccer, he practised his soccer skills with a tennis ball and waited for autumn, winter and spring – the real times of the year, the times when there was soccer.

Outside soccer, Danny lived an ordinary life. He went to school, came back again, ate, slept and messed about. He was a perfectly satisfactory sort of boy in all these occupations, who seldom caused trouble or felt troubled.

Now, he felt troubled. It was mid-evening. He was alone in the house and his parents would not return for another hour and a half – they were with neighbours, Mr and Mrs Elphin, three doors down the road. To reach his parents, Danny had only to pick up the telephone and dial a number he perfectly well knew, or go down the road and knock on a familiar door. He felt unable to do either of these things, however, for what was there to say when they answered? He imagined the conversation . . .

'Mum, there's something in the living-room.'

'What's in the living-room?'

'Something. You know, *something*.'

'Dad, speak to Danny, he's gone bonkers. He says there's "something" in the living-room.'

Dad speaking: 'What's all this, son?'

'It's the living-room. There's something *in* it . . .'

'Something in the living-room!' thought Danny; that wouldn't do for sensible people like his parents. 'And it won't do for me, either!' Danny said to himself. So he turned the TV volume knob down a bit, and looked more closely at the Something.

There it was again! Over there! It had moved. It was nearer the door, further away from the TV. As he watched, it moved again: the pattern on the carpet shifted and wavered, the legs of a chair went hazy and somehow muffled, the panels of the door went out of focus. There was a greyness. Danny picked up the heavy poker from the fireplace.

How big was the Something? Six feet, at least. Six feet of nothing-very-much, six feet of disturbance and slight darkness. Perhaps it was his own eyes? Danny looked at a picture on the wall: clear as a bell. He looked at the TV picture: clean, sharp, the same as usual. He looked at the Something: no, it wasn't his eyes.

And it was still moving! It was moving by the door, *through* the closed door! It was half out of the door and half in! No, it was coming back again, moving, still moving, moving very slowly.

Vaguely moving and wavering and flickering. But it was there all right.

Danny lifted the poker and brought it down, not hard, on the Something. He gave a sort of yelp, because he thought he had felt a semi-solid resistance to the blow. When the poker touched it, he thought the Something had flickered.

It moved away from him. He followed it and hit it again, harder.

A chair went over with a clatter. The Something had knocked it over, it must have done, he was nowhere near the chair. He hit it again. The Something moved on like a slug-shaped patch of mist, wavering, flickering, putting things out of focus, darkening the view. He hit it again, and again.

It was getting darker, he could almost see it. It was humped, long, legless, heaving, moving!

Suddenly Danny threw down the poker and ran out of the room. He ran upstairs to the bathroom, slammed the door and locked it. He stood by the door, listening, but all he could hear was his own panting breath. He went to the mirror on the wall and looked at himself. His white-faced reflection looked back at him, wide-eyed and worried. He put his tongue out: so did the face in the mirror. He said, 'Up the Arsenal!' and clasped his hands in a boxer's handshake: so did the Danny in the mirror.

He sighed, let out a long breath, turned on the cold tap and rinsed his face with a minimum of cold water. 'There you are, then!' he said cheerfully, 'You still don't like cold water, do you? Do you?' He and his reflection nodded and he carefully inspected the drops of water on his face before leaving the mirror and wiping the moisture off with a blue towel. Then he put his head against the door and listened. Not a sound.

He walked down the stairs slowly, listening to the TV set. It was saying, 'For the *real* flavour of *real* coffee –' then a girl's squeaky voice said, 'Reeelly?' Danny could see the advertisement in his mind. His lips formed the rest of the dialogue –

Down in the living-room, another chair went over.

He retreated three or four steps up the stairs, then checked himself. 'Go downstairs, Yellowbelly!' he said, out loud, and went down the stairs.

In the living-room there were now two chairs on their sides and the Something was still there, moving faster. It brushed against a little table and a plant in a pot went down with a crash. Danny picked up the poker and hit and hit and hit. Then the thing blundered against the TV set.

The set went down and there were flashes and a line of fire showing through the perforated guard at the back and then smoke and bursts and pops of fire. All the lights went out. As they went out, Danny saw it, almost completely! – the definite shape of the humps, the scarred texture of it, the livid crisscross that suddenly faded as the TV set went dead, the swing of what might have been a head! –

Then it came towards him, fast, and he kept hitting and hitting and hitting but it got him against the wall. He would have been crushed if it hadn't knocked the wall down. Danny fell through the great hole with all the lath and plaster.

By now he was screaming and the smoke was everywhere and the phone was ringing in the hall. He fell over something trying to reach the phone and landed flat on his face. He could feel *it* near him, he wanted to roll one way or another to get out of its way but the hall was very narrow and he didn't know which way it was coming –

Then the front door slammed open and his father was flicking light switches that didn't work. The phone kept ringing. His father got the big battery lantern from the hall cupboard and swung it round. He said, 'For God's sake . . .!' There was smoke and plaster dust everywhere, he didn't see Danny at first, he picked up the phone and said, 'Bob? Something's happened, it's a madhouse, yes, yes, ring you back!' Then he did see Danny and said, 'What the hell –' and knelt down beside his son as Danny's mother came rushing in.

Danny couldn't answer their questions at first. He could hear himself sobbing and whooping and hear them asking questions and the phone ringing again ('Mrs Elphin? Yes, something's happened, yes please, yes, come over right away') but he couldn't stop the noises he was making.

By the time he could talk and listen, Mrs Elphin from number fifty-seven was there and a policeman too. The lights were on again – his father had mended a fuse. The policeman was saying, 'When you get a dead short like that, the spark can jump and then the other fuses can blow. A dead short, you see.'

They made no sense of Danny's story. The two chairs, the little table, the plant pot, the TV set – they could understand them, but not the hole in the wall. Danny's mother began to repeat to herself, 'He's a *quiet* boy,' she said, 'Quiet. It's not as if he were, you know, *excitable*, he's a *quiet* boy . . .!' The policeman made notes, Mrs Elphin made tea and Danny's father made a face that meant 'we'll get to the bottom of this later, my lad.'

'I knew something was wrong,' said Mrs Elphin. 'I heard noises from *this* house when the Mathesons left *our* house . . . then all the lights going out . . . That's why I phoned, Officer.'

'A dead short,' said the policeman.

So they neither believed nor disbelieved Danny at the time. Later on, of course, they believed him.

Hoppicopter

An amazing Aston-Martin limousine, painted metallic gold, slithered like an exotic serpent down the modest road and settled, purring and whispering to itself, outside the Rideout's house.

From the amazing car emerged an amazing chauffeur: a girl. She wore a proper, old-fashioned chauffeur's peaked cap, brilliantly polished leather gaiters and a plum-coloured uniform. Her unnaturally blonde hair hung down to a waist encircled by a leather belt so tight that she appeared to be cut in two, like a wasp. Her heavily made-up blue eyes were like a doll's. Her small, scarlet mouth was doll-like too.

This chauffeur walked briskly to the Rideouts' front door, which was opened by Lucas. The chauffeur said, 'Rideouts?' and sniffed noisily. Lucas said, 'Yes.' The chauffeur said, in a strong Cockney accent, 'Gorrer fridge?' Lucas replied, 'A fridge? Have we got one? Yes.' He watched her, stunned, as she turned on her high heel, marched down the drive, opened the boot of the Aston-Martin and took out a hamper. 'Cop hold,' she said to Lucas. He helped her carry the leather-and-wicker hamper to the kitchen. Mrs Rideout watched in dumb amazement.

In the kitchen, the chauffeur sniffed violently through her little round nostrils, opened the hamper and said, 'Gorrer corkscrew?' Wide-eyed, Mrs Rideout offered the corkscrew. 'I forgorrer corkscrew,' the chauffeur explained. 'Goes spare when I forget fings, Doctor does. 'Ave my guts for garters.'

Expertly, she opened a wine bottle labelled Sancerre; put the bottle to her lips to take a small swig; made a disgusted face and swallowed; and said, "At'll do. Pop it in the fridge.'

Mrs Rideout, stunned, started to obey: then, collecting her wits, said, 'Wait a minute! Who *are* you?'

'Doctor Kalabza's chauffeur, o'course! 'E's coming 'ere! Didn'tcher know?'

'No.'

'Cor. Well, 'e likes 'is wine chilled.'

Lucas found courage to ask the chauffeur, 'Where's the doctor?' She pointed a red-nailed finger skywards and sniffed. 'In 'is 'oppicopter,' she explained. Lucas did not understand the explanation but was afraid to speak again. The glittering presence of the chauffeur in the everyday kitchen overwhelmed him. And anyway, the chauffeur was busy doing complicated things to little jars, tureens and terrines from the hamper. From a small stone bowl, she scooped a sample with her fingernail and gobbled it. 'Muck,' she said, and apparently satisfied, laid a tray. The tray was the inside of the hamper's lid and had a surface of smoked glass. Lucas wondered how much the hamper cost, and the little pots inside it. 'About five years' pocket money,' he concluded. But then he heard the noise in the sky outside, and went out to discover what caused it.

It was a very small red and white helicopter – the 'hoppicopter' the chauffeur had mentioned – over the field at the end of the road. He ran to see it land.

It took a long time descending, dipping and swaying and going up and down like a noisy yoyo.

The chauffeur was beside him now, watching. 'Kill 'imself,' she said, and gave a satisfied sniff. Then – 'Berrer meet 'im innis car, I spose.' She strode away on her over-long legs to get the Aston-Martin. Lucas went back to the house. He wanted to hide.

All too soon, the car was at the front door, the chauffeur announced, 'It's 'im' – and there stood Doctor Zafar Kalabza.

He stood lower than any of the Rideouts had imagined. TV makes famous people appear big. In fact, the Doctor was shorter than Lucas or Lettice – yet somehow enormous and room-filling, like sudden blazing sunlight. His golden-brown face was almost hidden by a huge bunch of radiant hot-house flowers. He peered from behind them with glittering dark eyes that darted from person to person – found the terrified Mrs Rideout – and cried, 'Darling Lady! Flowers! They match you exactly, I knew they would, they are yours!'

He pressed the flowers to Mrs Rideout's cardiganed bosom, raised his arms high above his head and shouted, 'Home! At last I feel I am at home! An English home! They say I am more English than the English, they are so right, only the English understand how to – Where is that stupid chauffeur girl, that Polly, where is my food? Polly! Here she comes, the dove, the throstle . . . put the tray down there. Ah, here is Mr Rideout, a scientific, a brother! I shake your hand! And now, food.'

The Doctor thrust himself at the food, cramming his mouth with spoonfuls from one little pot after another, pausing only to shout for wine. 'I'll bring it,' said Mrs Rideout, faintly, and got the bottle from the kitchen.

'Sancerre!' cried the Doctor. 'Oh, dear lady, how did you know? Empathy! Telepathy! Sancerre!'

'Actually, it was your chauffeur that brought it –' began

Mrs Rideout, but the Doctor was not listening. He flourished his white napkin, pushed little nuggets of expensive food into his mouth and bellowed, 'But to business! Waste not a moment! Where is she? Where is the enchantress, the so-gifted one, the holder of the key, the moulder of destinies? Where is Lettice? Polly, stop sniffing, you disgust me! It is her septum, Mr Rideout – the little bone in the nose, Mrs Rideout – take away this tray, I am finished, you must undergo surgery, Polly, a very minor operation, I will arrange everything – Lettice, where is Lettice?'

Lettice, scarlet-faced, was pushed forward. She towered above the Doctor as a dockside crane looms over a racing yacht.

'So!' shouted the Doctor, seizing Lettice as if he would climb up her and kissing her loudly, twice, once on each cheek – 'So! It is she! The little fair lady with the fair name, Lettice! I love you, Lettice! And you shall love me! Waste not a moment! Sit beside me, dearest Lettice and tell me of your talks with the animals! Wine, wine, first take some wine!'

He thrust a glass of Sancerre at Lettice's stiff lips. '*I* cannot talk to the animals, dearest girl, I can only listen, sometimes, to their voices . . . To the dolphins, and the singing whales, did you know they sing, Lettice? And sometimes I listen to the brain itself –'

'I know,' Lettice muttered. 'You use those machines with electrodes. You tie them down, the poor animals, and drug them and scrape patches of fur off them –'

'To receive the language of the brain!' cried the Doctor, hearing nothing Lettice said. 'So very beautiful! But so puzzling for your poor friend the Doctor, who seeks to know all and knows – poof! – nothing!'

Lettice stared disgustedly ahead of herself, feeling her face begin to sweat. The Doctor thought she was looking at the string of beads round his neck – strange beads, not really beads at all, little images and emblems.

'Ah, dearest girl, I see your eyes are drawn to my necklace! You understand, of course you understand, are we not twin souls? Yes, perhaps these little beads contain the secret we both seek! Here are Amrithar and Thoth-ge, and Sambiranda the All-wise, whose kingdom was ruled by the Guardian Cats!'

Lettice's expression was such that even the Doctor noticed it. 'Or perhaps they are just silly little carvings,' he said; 'carvings that bore you. Ah, dear Lettice, forgive me – look, I am putting them away, hiding them in my shirt – for you are of today, Lettice, you wish to talk of science, the newest and greatest science, the science of the mind, the perceptions! Your science, Lettice!'

'You shouldn't do experiments on animals,' muttered Lettice, almost speechless with dislike and embarrassment. 'It's horrible.'

For a moment, the Doctor was stopped short. In that moment, Lucas thought he saw the computer-fast workings of the Doctor's mind – its lightning reception of facts, its instant Go/No-go decisions, the expert and in this case damning judgement of himself, the determination to bounce back and win the next round.

'Chess!' shouted the Doctor, jumping to his feet and removing himself from Lettice. 'I see a chessboard! We shall play, Mr Rideout! Immediately!'

'I play too,' Lucas said.

'I will play you both at once!' said the Doctor. 'It is easier for me, I am so very impatient – and I have a board. Polly, get the little chess set from the car, do not sniff, such an ugly habit – it is in the locker facing the front seats – quickly –'

An hour and a half later, five simultaneous games had

been played. The Doctor played like a pouncing tiger, with perfectly controlled ferocity. He beat Mr Rideout five times out of five and Lucas four times.

'You let me win that game,' Lucas complained.

'Win, lose,' said the Doctor, flourishing an arm. 'What does it matter? Or perhaps it matters a great deal. Always there is this matter of win and lose. In all games it is the same, don't you think so, Lettice? Win or Lose, Live or Die. There is no escaping it, Lettice. Is there?'

'Why ask me?' Lettice said, not looking at the Doctor.

'Oh, but Lettice, think! Here are the animals, your lovely animals, doing strange things all over the world. Such strange games they play . . . What are we to make of them? Tell us, Lettice! What is the game?'

'I don't know,' Lettice muttered. 'Not chess, anyway.'

'And you don't want to know, Lettice. Because of the other games, the cruel games men play with animals. Vivisection, so ugly a word and so ugly an act. You would never play that game, Lettice.'

She looked at him sullenly and said, '*You* would.'

Her father said, 'But he never has, Lettice. Have you, Doctor?'

'"Scientist" is a dirty word to our Lettice,' said the Doctor. Lucas noticed that he was speaking quietly now, for the first time. It was as if he had changed gear; as if his gaudy clothes, even, had suddenly become serious and sombre; as if he radiated the authority of sheer intelligence. 'A dirty word, "scientist", is that it, Lettice? Or is she the new scientist herself? The greatest scientist? Because she speaks to the animals, the animals who are playing such a strange game.' He leaned forward, making her look at him. 'Do you speak to animals, Lettice?'

'Yes . . . No. I think so. In a way. I don't know.'

'You *do* know, Lettice. And you must tell me.'

'Why should I tell you?' she said, staring him full in the face.

'Because of the game, Lettice. The new game the animals have invented. We must join together to find out what sort of game it is. Is it a game of jolly fun, between friends? Do you think it is, Lettice? I see you do not. Your face tells me. Is it a game of Win or Lose, quite serious but not a war? Or is it, do you think, a game of conquer or perish, Live or Die?'

'All this talk of win or lose, conquer or die,' Lettice began, floundering, 'It isn't like that at all! You've got it all wrong in your mind!'

'Go on.'

'It's not the *animals*. They're not doing it, they're not doing anything! It's *them*! *They* are doing it. Doing it to the animals!'

'Them? They?'

'The Blobs, the big shapes they see and we can't see! That's the important thing to find out about! The animals don't matter. Find out about the Blobs and you'd have the answer to everything!'

'Does this answer matter very much, Lettice? Is it a case of Win or Lose, or is it Live or Die?'

'How do I know? Why ask me?'

'I ask you because you are the only one to ask,' said the Doctor. 'You say the animals are merely witnesses in the case, is that right? You are the only one who speaks the language of the witnesses, Lettice! Only you! So tell me, you must tell me: is there a criminal in the case? Is there a crime? What have the witnesses been saying to you, Lettice?'

She stood up, her mouth working. 'You just talk and talk!' she burst out. 'You don't *understand* ... And *I* understand ... ' She was almost in tears. 'Nobody takes any notice of me!' she accused. 'Everyone just laughs and – and jeers – and makes fun . . .'

'Is there a criminal? Is there a crime?' the Doctor insisted. 'Name it, Lettice! Name it!'

'Television!' she said. The word burst out of her. '*Television*! Oh, it's so obvious, they've *told* me about it . . . Catchmouse, poor old Duff, frightened out of their wits . . . It's *television*!'

Suddenly she'd had enough. She ran upstairs, the door of her bedroom slammed. Mrs Rideout came in, her face twisted with worry. 'Oh, dear!' she said. 'I hope she wasn't rude –'

'I think I know what she meant,' Doctor Kalabza said. Yet again, Lucas seemed to see the stern computer behind the gaudy mask. 'I think she means Raster.'

Raster

'Raster?' Lucas said. He was alone with the Doctor now. 'What is Raster?'

The chauffeur, Polly, bustled in before the Doctor could reply. She slapped a tray of delicacies and a glass of white wine in front of the Doctor, and said, 'There you are then. I'm off.'

'Off? Where off?' said the Doctor.

'Have a swim. I can be down at the coast in twenty-five minutes.'

'But dear good girl! – I do not pay you to take my car and go swimming –' began the Doctor. Polly simply said, 'That's all right, then,' and left.

'It's always like that,' said the Doctor, rolling his eyes. 'They despise me because I am physically small, you see. Take my advice, dear Lucas: grow up to be big. A six-footer, definitely. Even two metres will not be too much in the near future. People are growing all the time, did you know that? King Arthur and his knights, were, what is the word, titchy.'

'I might not grow up at all,' said Lucas stiffly. He wished the Doctor would not clown.

'But why not, dear friend?'

'The things Lettice calls Blobs. And the animals going mad. It might be the end of our world. The Blobs and the animals might make it impossible for us to live in our own world.'

'Tck, tck, tck!' said the Doctor. 'That is a counsel of despair, is it not? But of course you are not serious. The great plagues that decimated our civilizations, the scourges and upheavals and wars and weapons – they come, they go. Mankind survives.'

'But how can we live with the Blobs?'

'How can we fail to live with them? What alternative is there? We will learn about these Blobs; understand them, control them, conquer them!'

'But suppose we *don't*!'

'Compromise,' said the Doctor.

'What do you mean, compromise?'

'Compromise. Make different arrangements. Live and let live. Peaceful co-existence. Any phrase you like, dear Lucas, that means sharing this planet with a new tribe, these Blobs.'

'But suppose they won't let us share! Suppose they want everything!'

'Then we would make a move away, like moving house. There will always be regions, in this planet or another, where the Blobs do not occur. The sky is full of planets!'

'But that could take centuries. Suppose we have to move fast, move now!'

'Suppose, suppose, suppose!' laughed the Doctor. 'Here is a glass of wine, it can do you no harm. Drink!'

Lucas said, 'Cheers,' in a dismal voice, and drank the wine. Then he remembered something. 'Raster,' he said. 'You said "Raster". What does it mean?'

'Ah!' said the Doctor dramatically, at his worst again. 'All will be revealed! – tonight! – on your television set!'

The Rideouts switched on the set, settled themselves in their chairs, and waited to be amazed. 'Here he comes!' said Lucas. And there he was: beaming, gaudy, cocksure.

Everyone else seemed so normal compared with the Doctor. And his TV manner was appalling.

'. . . an opportunity to welcome a man celebrated in at least four scientific fields,' began Ivor Mitcham, the host of the show.

'Five,' said the Doctor, stopping Ivor Mitcham in his tracks.

'I'm sorry . . .?'

'Five scientific fields,' said the Doctor. 'Five I am celebrated in, not four.'

'Five it is, Doctor Kalabza, five it is. And now –'

'And now,' said the Doctor, taking over, 'let us talk about the so strange behaviour of the animals! And about the Blobs, as a friend of mine calls them. A very particular friend: a young lady, a blonde young lady!' He rolled his eyes roguishly at the cameras.

'Oh!' cried Lettice. '*Oh*!'

She heard little more of the programme. Fury made her face burn and her mind churn. She did not properly hear the Doctor talk of animals or Blobs.

Neither did the studio audience. A white-haired man in the second row of the audience kept barking 'Nonsense!' 'Prove it!' 'Unscientific!' A woman at the back produced a poster reading:

SAVE THE ANIMALS
ALL GOD'S CREATURES

She shouted something in a strangled, high-pitched voice that no one could understand. Ivor Mitcham busily kept smiling. The Doctor kept moving, bobbing up and down, kicking the table with his toe so that the microphone picked up a drum sound.

'*Raster*!' said the Doctor, loudly and suddenly.

'What was that?' said Ivor Mitcham.

'Raster, my friend. That could be the answer, do you not think? I think so. My very young blonde lady friend thinks so. It may be so, do you not think?'

'I'm sorry, Doctor, I don't know this Raster –'

'My dear good friend, you *are* Raster! And me! And our friends in the audience! But most of all, dear Mr Michelin, *this* is Raster!' - and the Doctor lunged forward and poked a finger at the lens of a TV camera.

The picture on the Rideouts' screen darkened as the approaching finger became a great obscuring blur. There was confusion for a moment in the studio until the director cued in another camera. Then the Doctor could be seen, smiling broadly, apparently tickling the lens of a camera. One of the crew was flapping at his hand trying to get rid of him. Ivor Mitcham was pulling at the Doctor's free arm.

The programme settled down again. The screen was filled with videotapes showing animals behaving strangely. Ivor Mitcham's voice gave a commentary. There was nothing very surprising in the clips – the world was used to freakish animal behaviour by now – until there was a brief shot that showed something truly unpleasant.

A field of woolly sheep . . . their heads lifted as if at some signal . . . the sheep move back uneasily, jostling each other, coming nearer to the camera . . . some sheep are jostled and fall from the flock but rejoin it . . . three sheep lose their nerve and break away, running towards the camera – and then a sequence almost indecent in its unlikeliness; the sheep face the camera, looking at a point to one side of it – their lips raise and wrinkle, their eyes roll – and then the long yellow teeth are bared, the terrified animals are snarling at something. Sheep, snarling!

In the studio, there was a shocked 'Ooooo – oh!' from the audience; the same sound the Rideouts made at home. Sheep, snarling!

Doctor Kalabza's face filled the screen. It was alert, unemotional, fascinated. Ivor Mitcham said, 'Well, Doctor Kalabza, what do you make of that?'

'My dear friend, it is nothing new, there are many such incidents . . . Over the whole world we hear of such things. Even the sheep –'

'But what do you think it is, Doctor Kalabza?'

'I have told you. It is Raster.'

'Raster, Doctor?'

'The name given to the patterns formed by the television transmissions which themselves form the pictures on our television screens. That is Raster, my friend. You should know that, being in the industry of television.'

'And Raster accounts for the behaviour of those sheep?'

'Oh no, certainly not that, not at all! But I have a belief that Raster explains the behaviour of the phenomenon that causes the behaviour of the sheep.'

'*Nonsense*!' said the white-haired man in the audience. '*Unscientific*!' The camera picked him out. A military-looking man, peppery and impatient; but not a crank.

'*Chemicals*!' he shouted. 'Never mind Raster. Chemicals. Pollution. Chemicals. Fertilizers, antibiotics, genetic manipulation, pesticides! Chemicals!'

People in the audience were standing up and shouting. Most of them seemed to be supporting the peppery man but the woman with the placard was hooting something about 'all creatures great and small . . .' It was getting very noisy again.

'Chemicals! Poisons! Driving the animals mad!'

'Save the poor dumb creatures! Save them, save them!'

The programme director lost control. Shot after shot came on the screen, face after face. Then the woman with the poster put things in focus by fainting.

Now the cameras had something to hold on to. They showed unlikely pictures of her being passed over the heads of the audience. Her poster followed her, passed from hand to hand.

Ivor Mitcham's face filled the screen. His smile was as perfect as ever. 'Well, there you are,' he said, 'the animals are behaving oddly. Even the *human* animals!'

'Wrong about Raster,' shouted the Major. 'Chemicals and poisons.'

'You should meet,' the Doctor shouted back, roguishly wagging a finger, 'my little blonde lady. She would tell you most differently, my friend!'

'BRING HER ON!' shouted a voice from the audience. People laughed and applauded. Ivor Mitcham said, 'Well . . .? Can you produce the lady, Doctor?'

'Of course!' said the Doctor. 'At any time!'

In the Rideout living room, Lettice let out a scandalized, agonized 'Ooooh!'

It was almost as if Doctor Kalabza's television appearance had acted as a trigger mechanism for an international bomb. Next day, from all over the world, the reports came in. The Blobs were on the rampage. They were running wild. And they were, increasingly, becoming visible.

In the small town where the Rideouts lived, there were enough Blob stories to fill the next edition of the local newspaper – not that the townspeople needed to wait for the newspaper; they told each other their strange tales.

In the supermarket: 'First it was my new kitchen units, you know, the ones Rod put in only two weekends ago – well, they're all smashed and ruined now, you've never seen anything like it, this great sort of wobbly shape going around just smashing and bashing and knocking all the fronts in, the whole lot's just matchwood now, and Rod put in so much work . . . Well, I just sat down when it was all over and I just cried and cried, I couldn't help myself . . .'

In a pub: 'So when I get home, that would be twenty minutes after closing time, not late, I slip the key in the door quiet-like, you know, and I hear the missus up the top of the stairs in the dark and she's shouting and cursing. "Oh, you drunken beast!" she says, "Oh, I'll kill you for this tomorrow, see if I don't!" and suchlike. So I just stand there with the key in my hand, wondering what she's on about. I mean, I'm not drunk and it's not late . . .

'Then I hear this thumping and bumping and crashing in the lounge and I goes in to see what's up and switch on the light but there isn't any light – and *there it is*, blobby like they tell you and all striped, lurching round the room and breaking everything. So I back out, sharpish, and creep up the stairs, and when I get to the top – she lets out a great scream and says, "Oh, Tom! It's you! I mean, it wasn't you!" And then she passes out cold, and who's to blame her?'

In a hospital: 'No, *you* listen to *me*, Constable! I was driving buses before you got issued your first pair of size thirteens! – No, *listen*, and write it down in your little notebook. Right, we're approaching the request stop at Shadbrook Road and the Library, right? And no other traffic and the road's clear, but it's dark, right? And I'm already slowing down a bit, to say twenty-five, because I think I see people at the stop, right? But I don't see people at all, it's one of them Blobs, and I hit it with my nearside front, and that sends us right across to the wrong side of the road, right? – and that's when we roll over, and I get this broken arm, and lucky it wasn't my neck, a smash like that, right? Now, you got that all written down?'

In a school playground: 'They're all trampled flat, Dad's cabbages, and all the bean poles snapped off too. It was trying to get in again, see. Through the back door. It went out the side door – went right through it – and then it was the dustbins, one of them's squashed almost flat. And I could see the stripes, like it says on the telly. It smashed the telly first go off. It was like a big see-through slug, you know, no proper shape at all, just something big and humpy. You ought to see the front room, it's fantastic. Stripes? No, no stripes . . . Not after it smashed the telly . . .

'Know what, I never thought of that! Once it had smashed the telly, it didn't have stripes! I mean, that's the first thing I'd have noticed when it was rooting about in the garden in the dark. I'd have noticed the stripes, they sort of flicker. But after it'd done up the telly, there weren't any stripes on it . . .'

Lettice and Miss Langham looked at each other across the pale oak table in the school library room and, simultaneously, shrugged. Then they laughed because neither had known the other was about to shrug. Lettice was, for a moment, surprised to find herself laughing with Miss Langham: their relationship these days seemed very easy and casual, almost friendly.

'There's no point in this any more,' said Miss Langham, pointing to the fat scrapbooks they had been working on. 'There's simply too much material. Too many Blobs reported from too many countries, too many reports and stories.'

'We're just keeping the scrapbooks for the sake of it,' Lettice agreed. 'They don't *mean* anything anymore. Besides, we've been doing it all wrong.'

'What do you mean?'

'Well, when we started, every story we pasted in the books seemed . . . significant. As if it might prove something. But now –'

'Now your case is proved. Proved a million times.'

'I wasn't trying to score a point, I just meant . . . Miss Langham, our books aren't any good because they don't make the *difference*.'

'What difference?'

'The difference between the stories about Blobs and the stories about animals.'

'You mean, we should have started out to keep one set of books for Blobs, and the other for Animals? Yes, I see. But why is it important?'

'What I mean is, the animals are familiar things behaving in a funny way. But the Blobs are unfamiliar, new things. Oh dear, I don't really know what I mean. Except that animals are animals, Blobs are Blobs!' said Lettice, helplessly.

'But the animals didn't start behaving oddly until the Blob business started. So surely the two things are connected?'

'Connected, but not the same. And now they're not even always connected. I mean, the things that happened here in our own town, last night – they didn't have anything to do with animals, did they?'

'No,' said Miss Langham. 'You're perfectly right. They didn't. It was all Blobs. So you're trying to say – now, the Blobs are on their own? But there are still stories from all over the place about animals doing strange things. That zoo in Berlin –'

'Oh, don't, it's awful, it's dreadful! Those poor monkeys!'

'And the poor keepers . . .? One was killed, you know. Torn to pieces by gibbons.'

'Oh, don't!' repeated Lettice. There had been a photograph in the newspaper of a cluster of gibbons, like swarming bees, forming a knot in one corner of the cage. Invisible in the centre of that knot there had been a man, imprisoned against the bars by hundreds of little hands – hands that were pulling the man to pieces. The man was dead now and so were the gibbons. In her mind's eye, she saw the other newspaper photographs: keepers with rifles braced against iron bars. And one grainy photograph of a gibbon falling backwards from the pattern of bars and mesh at the top of the cage: falling spreadeagled, clutching at nothing. This was the picture she could not forget. 'Why,' she asked herself, 'why that picture? Why aren't I haunted by that poor keeper that was killed? He was a human being, like me.'

Lettice looked down at her own body. It was changing fast. Her arms were rounder now. Her hands were no longer bony, the unbitten nails were oval. Her thighs were rounder, her knees no longer raw-looking. 'I'm growing up!' she thought. 'Then why can't I think like a grown-up? As if all the gibbons in the world mattered as much as one man!'

But she could not convince herself.

Miss Langham, she realized, was still looking at the press cuttings and talking about them. Lettice shook herself to attention.

'. . . very important indeed,' said Miss Langham crisply. 'You are quite right – the two subjects, the animals and the Blobs, *need not* be related now, even if they were related in the first place. I wonder . . .'

'Animals – afraid of the Blobs – animals angry: Blobs – fear of television – Blobs angry,' said Lettice, startled by her own precision and decisiveness. 'That's what I think is happening.'

'But even if you're right,' said Miss Langham, 'what do we *do*? Doctor Kalabza –'

'Oh, wonderful Doctor Kalabza!' snapped Lettice. 'He's coming back soon and he'll start all over again being –'

'Being impossible and embarrassing?'

'Yes.'

'And right about everything?'

'Yes! I mean, no. Oh, I don't know. He's so *awful*. And yet . . .'

'And *yet*. I know exactly what you mean.' Miss Langham smiled ruefully. 'He'll turn out to be right, Lettice. He always is.'

'Well,' Lettice said, 'he's certainly not right about me appearing on TV! I couldn't! Not ever!'

Lettice on TV

'I think you're being very silly,' Mrs Rideout told Lettice. 'I mean, it's the chance of a lifetime! You can't just say, "I can't, I'm too shy" –'

'But I *am* shy,' said Lettice. 'I mean, appearing on television! Me! It's all right for you and all the neighbourhood, you don't have to *do* it. And I don't see why I should!'

'And there's your friends at school,' added Mrs Rideout. 'What will they say if you don't appear? After all . . . all *this*?' She pointed a finger at the pile of press cuttings on the table by the sofa.

There were dozens of them each day; ever since Dr Kalabza's TV appearance. 'THE BLONDE AND THE BLOBS –DOES LITTLE LETTICE HOLD THE CLUE?' . . . 'BEAUTY AND THE BEASTS' . . . 'SHE TALKS WITH THE ANIMALS: WHEN WILL SHE TALK TO US?' Mrs Rideout collected the cuttings, cut them out neatly and stuck them in a large scrapbook with a paste that smelled of cloves.

All this sickened Lettice, as did the journalists who kept ringing the front door bell. Lettice hid, but it did no good. Her mother told the journalists, 'I know she's somewhere around, she was in here only a minute ago . . . Lettice! *Lettice!*' (this in her mother's special, ladylike, cooing, all-happy-family voice). 'Do come down, dear! Some gentlemen here *particularly* want to meet you!'

Almost always, Lettice would have to go down and meet the journalists; feeling a fool, looking a fool and muttering words that she knew to be foolish as they left her mouth.

And now they wanted her to make a fool of herself on television! 'I won't!' said Lettice. 'I won't and that's final!'

Nevertheless, two weeks later, she found herself sitting in the large limousine sent by the TV company, with her brother, mother and father. She was on her way to the television studio – Doctor Kalabza would be there – to make her starring appearance in *Fenton's Forum*, the biggest talk show of them all.

She felt little or nothing of their reception at the TV centre – only a dim consciousness of blue lights from camera flash-guns – of her mother's fixed smile and constant glow of maternal delight – of her father's insistence on knowing, precisely, the names of everyone introduced to the Rideouts ('You're who? What? Jamie Sinclair? Jamie? No, doesn't ring a bell. Programme Director? What's that? Oh, I see. No, wait a minute, I don't quite see . . .')

At last, after a long period of sitting in a small cell like a shrunken hotel room, she was taken to a sort of dentist's chair. A make-up girl called Fiona put a towel round her neck. Fiona was quick, clever, and heavily and excellently made up. 'Big pores here, luv,' she said, touching Lettice's nose. 'Fill 'em in with goo. There. Gone.' She dabbed and smeared away industriously at Lettice's face, which slowly became almost unrecognizable to Lettice.

'Split ends,' she said, holding up a lock of Lettice's hair. 'Me too. I've tried egg, beer rinses, everything. No flipping good.'

In another chair, the famous face of a current-events commentator was being seen to by a girl called Tricia. The famous face's eyes were closed and the famous nose was snoring very slightly. 'He shouldn't be here,' Fiona said, 'but I don't dare wake him. *Scenes.* You are the one that talks to the animals?'

'Yes,' said Lettice. 'That is –'

'You should talk to him, then!' said Fiona. 'Real old beast, he is! Free with his hands. There you are, luv. All done and wiped. Whatever you do, *don't touch.*'

Lettice said, 'Oh, you mean –' and touched her face.

Fiona pounced on her, dabbed at the mark Lettice had made and said, 'That's what I specially don't want you to do, luv. *Right?* Right.'

And somehow Lettice found herself in a studio. She was so busy telling herself not to touch herself – under the hot and brilliant lights, she could feel sweat trying to make its way through the make-up – that she heard or sensed nothing at all of what was going on. She was being rehearsed, they told her. It meant nothing.

Then suddenly the programme was live! – on the air! – actually happening! – and Larry Fenton was poking his face at her across the chrome and glass table with the microphones on it, and asking her a question.

'I'm sorry . . .?' she blurted, overwhelmed by several things all at once – the piercing eyes of Mr Fenton, glittering with intelligence, warmth, interest and a sort of knowing inner depth of ruthlessness and self-love; the sickening lurch of a TV camera, its lens pointing straight at every nerve end in her body; Doctor Kalabza, much too at ease, smiling encouragingly; the perpetual smile on her mother's face, showing white in the blur of the audience; and the utter hopelessness of her own position. She was lost. Completely lost.

'. . . in other words, Lettice, you are able to *converse* with animals?' said Larry Fenton. Seeing that Lettice was still incapable of answering, he added, 'I mean, not converse *rationally*, with *words*, but attain a degree of *communication* . . .?'

'I don't mind this choking,' thought Lettice – her throat was stuffed with a ball of wool and her ears seemed to be hissing and Mr Fenton's face was swelling before her eyes – 'But why can't I die? Why don't I die?'

At this moment, there was a thump and a scuffle in the audience – a ripple of exclamations, a sudden yell and some high pitched shouting – a camera lurched and its operator swore and fell to one side – and the big, dark, wavering shapes were thrusting and plunging in the studio.

The Blobs had come.

Larry Fenton was the quickest to react. He grabbed Lettice by the wrist and pulled her to a clear place. With his other hand, he made furious signals to the control room which overlooked the studio behind a flat, darkly glimmering plate-glass wall. Figures were bobbing up and down in the control room. Larry Fenton shouted, 'Keep it live, for God's sake, keep it live! You! Back on your camera! Keep shooting!' A young cameraman shouted 'O.K., O.K.!' and his camera moved about like a Dalek. The noise and confusion were getting worse.

A big blurred shape heaved against a lamp pillar and the falling lights exploded. A woman began to scream. 'Mother?' thought Lettice. 'No, there she is!' Her mother and father were trying to make their way to Lettice, but there were overturned chairs and lumpy Blob shapes and heaving knots of people in the way. For a moment, Lettice's and her mother's eyes met: incredibly, her mother switched on the social smile.

Now Doctor Kalabza had Lettice's other wrist and was shouting something in her ear. She felt absurd. The Doctor was tugging her one way, and Mr Fenton the other. 'What?' she yelled. 'What? I can't *hear* you! Oh, do leave go!'

Then her father got to her, his face set in very much its

usual inquiring, quizzical expression, but with a malicious twinkle underneath. He took hold of Larry Fenton's free hand, shook it and said, 'Very nice programme. What's on next?' Fenton was sufficiently taken aback to drop Lettice's wrist. 'Must dash,' said Mr Rideout, and led Lettice away, with the Doctor dangling behind.

Slowly the family linked up and found the way out. They turned and looked back.

The whole studio was being churned by the Blobs. Larry Fenton still held a hand microphone and was still talking into it. A big board with a stylized picture of the world on it suddenly cracked, fell and crumbled noisily as a Blob trampled it. Another Blob, heaving and turning, was making a snake-pit of cables around itself. There was a bang and a mauve flash, and the crisscross pattern on the Blob brightened for a moment. Then blue and mauve and yellow electric flashes began to invade one corner of the studio, as if someone had thrown fireworks – firemen were rushing down the corridor – people were stampeding for the exits. The Rideouts and Doctor Kalabza got out of the way.

Twenty minutes later, in the hospitality room, Lettice asked the Doctor, 'What were you trying to say to me?'

'I thought, dear child, that one of the Blobs had features,' said the Doctor, 'You know, almost a face. A snout, a place for ears and eyes, perhaps . . .? I was hoping you had seen something similar?' He was at his most serious.

'Oh,' said Lettice. 'No, I didn't see anything like that.'

'Perhaps I was mistaken,' said Doctor Kalabza. 'Even the Doctor makes mistakes.' Some excited TV people burst in, making apologetic noises. '*Not*,' said the Doctor, out-shouting them, '*Not*,' he claimed, deliberately becoming the flash celebrity, 'that your good friend the Doctor would make such a mistake as this.' He held up his glass. 'A *horrible* wine. A *deadly* wine . . .'

Miss Langham's Encounter

Next day, the newspaper headlines were all about Blobs. The television story was prominent but had to share space with similar reports from all over the world.

At school, the girls rushed up to Lettice and drowned her in questions. She barely heard them, for someone had told her that Miss Langham had had an accident and was in hospital. Lettice left school without another word and went to see her.

The Sister said, 'Only ten minutes. No more, mind.'

It was a little ward. There were only two beds in it. One was empty. In the other was Miss Langham, hidden by a curtain except for an arm and hand.

Lettice was reassured by the hand. It was so unmistakably Ann Langham's hand, smooth, neat. Lettice moved forward, said, 'Hello, Ann, it's me, Lettice,' and pulled aside the curtain.

The first shock was Ann's sleeping face. The plasters and bandages were bad enough – but the face was worse, swollen and blotched, misshapen and pulpy, with a short line of hideous black stitches running upwards from one side of the mouth.

Lettice gulped, repeated her 'Hello' and got her second shock.

Ann's eyes opened, took in Lettice's presence – and stared wildly. Her uninjured arm went up as if to ward off a blow.

Her voice said, loudly and harshly, *'Don't! Don't let them!'*

A moment later Ann was properly awake and herself again. She said, 'I'm all right really, I'm just in a sort of mess, that's all. I look much worse than I am, ask the Sister.'

'Doesn't it hurt you to speak?'

'Oddly enough, no. You see, Lettice,' (Lettice noticed, with amusement, the schoolmistress tone in her voice), 'in speaking one moves one's lower lip far more than one's upper.'

'Unless you're French, of course.'

'Unless you're French,' agreed Miss Langham; then, seeing how ridiculous the conversation had become, she laughed and hurt her mouth very much indeed. Lettice flustered around her trying to be helpful; and when the flurry was over, they felt close and companionable.

'I'm so glad *you've* come,' said Ann, touching Lettice's hand for an instant with her own. 'You're the only person I feel capable of talking to about that day. That Thursday evening . . . I was in my digs, doing the homework corrections. By some extraordinary coincidence, I was just picking your work up Lettice, when it started happening . . .'

'The Blobs?'

'The Blobs. Bumps and thumps. They'd arrived. Anyhow, I kept on with my work, thinking how awful your handwriting still is –'

'I know,' groaned Lettice.

'When just like that, the whole wall fell in on me. Well, it didn't fall: it was pushed. And there they were, two of them, two great Blobs covered all over with a grid of flickering lines. They started lurching about breaking everything . . .

'Oddly enough, Lettice, I didn't really mind this too much. The Blob thing can happen to anyone, and now it was happening to me and all one need do is keep out of harm's way and watch them smashing up the place. Which they did very thoroughly. By the time they were halfway through, I suddenly realized that the television was on in Josie's room – she's the girl who shares with me, she'd gone to the launderette and left the set on. I realized it, I may say, because the Blobs had by now removed the wall between my room and hers! Anyhow, I switched off the set and the Blobs didn't flicker quite so much. No stripes. Then the really unpleasant part started . . .

'The Blobs began behaving a little differently – more slowly, less actively destructive. They just stood in what remained of the room, lurching and flickering and nosing about.'

'Did they have noses, then?'

'Funny you should ask that. Yes, I began to think I could see some sort of features . . . nothing definite, just a feeling of – of ugly features; thick snouts; dull, hidden eyes . . . I don't know, I don't know.' She fell silent and looked out of the window.

When she spoke again it was in her best schoolmistress voice. 'You must understand, Lettice, that, until that very moment, I had regarded the Blobs as . . . as senseless, unpleasant, ugly, mobile *things*. Merely things. But now I was made to realize that the Blobs are not impersonal things after all. They have their own intentions and they make decisions.'

'How do you know that?'

'Because,' said Ann Langham, 'they positively and definitely attacked *me*. They more or less put their heads together and seemed to come to some decision.'

'What decision?'

'To beat me up,' said Miss Langham. 'They took a sort of run at me, one on either side . . . I got out of the way, the first time. But they kept on doing it – kept on lurching towards me and trying to trap me between them and pushing and shoving and moving forward. Deliberately. Wanting to hurt me . . .

'Anyhow, they got me down on the floor, and I think that's when I got some ribs cracked. It was very painful so naturally I tried to get up. But they wouldn't let me. They more or less hovered about above me, both of them, like great wavering balloons of *dark*, and they kept nudging me down to the floor again. I became rather frightened . . .'

'*Rather* frightened!' Lettice exclaimed. 'I'd have screamed my head off! What did you do?'

'Screamed my head off!' Ann confessed, 'to begin with. But it hurt my ribs. I seem to remember crying for a considerable period of time. I even swore. It was all rather pointless, I'm afraid. Not at all,' she added, with an attempt at a joke, 'what I would have expected of me!

'They stood over me, the Blobs,' Ann continued, 'not doing anything in particular but not letting me get up. Then I heard hammering at the door of our flat. It was a policeman, the people next door had reported the rumpus. He was hammering away and I was shouting, "The key is on the ledge over the door!" but he was hammering so loudly that he couldn't hear me. I suppose,' said Ann wanly, 'it was quite funny, really.'

'Uproarious,' said Lettice, taking Ann's hand. It trembled.

'At last,' Ann went on, 'the policeman heard me and took the key – Josie really shouldn't leave it there, but it was fortunate this time – and came to rescue me. But he simply couldn't reach me. The Blobs wanted to finish me off, it seemed. He could reach my hand and he tugged away at that, but the more he pulled, the more heavily they leaned in on me. And I swear they do have faces, Lettice! Faces of a sort . . . snouts, eyes . . . But all vague and flickering . . .'

She began to cry. Lettice said, 'This isn't doing you any good.'

'No, I will finish. The policeman was as desperate as I was. He kept saying, "Miss, what can I *do*?" – he always called me "miss" – but all I could do was scream, because I could feel my ribs trying to snap and my ankle was trapped. They injured it quite a bit, did I tell you? Anyhow, it went on and on until Josie came home and she and the policeman had the brilliant idea of switching on the television and bringing it very close to the Blobs. Apparently the luminous pattern, what Doctor Kalabza calls "Raster", began flickering all over their bodies – and the Blobs started to heave about and lurch this way and that to get away from the television radiation. I think they became striped, I can't remember. Anyhow, I got clear at last and here I am.'

The Sister opened the door and said, 'Out. You've stayed too long. O-u-t.'

Lettice rose. Ann said, 'Oh, Lettice, there's one thing more that you ought to know, and tell other people.'

'What?'

'Hate,' said Ann. 'The Blobs hate us, Lettice. Warn people.'

It turned out that there was no need, after all, for Lettice to deliver the message. During the next twenty-four hours, the Blobs made everything perfectly clear in every corner of the world.

In New York, the Brooklyn gang lost two of its members when a wall on the seventh storey of a tenement house exploded outwards, as if there had been a bomb inside the building. Several tons of brick, plaster and furniture smashed down on the flight of steps leading to the front door. The gang had been sitting on the steps. Merv and Little Pete died instantly. The 'bomb' was Blobs.

In Warsaw, Mrs and Mr Breslaw at last agreed about the Devil.

They were queueing together for a tram. When it came, the Breslaws elbowed and shoved and swore their way to the second of the tram's three steps. They were jam-packed in a press of people. So they never really saw what hit the tram and themselves. They heard the screams, felt the unbearable force of bodies, knew that the tram was swaying and toppling – but they could not see the wavering grey shapes crushing them because the shapes were behind their backs and there was no longer room in the crush even to turn one's head.

'It's the Devil!' screamed old Mr Breslaw, before the huge pressure of the Blobs flattened his lungs and stopped his heart.

'With you, it is always the Devil!' shouted his wife. But then she saw what was happening to her husband and knew it must happen to her. And with her last breath, she cried, 'You are right! You were always right! The Devil, the Devil, the Devil is come!'

In London, Doctor Kalabza was faded out in the middle of a TV chat show. He was warming up nicely when things went wrong – leaving his chair, walking about out of camera range, interrupting everyone, and even, when a dull speaker went on too long, performing elaborate exercises. Then the picture broke up, screens filled with snow and zigzags – and that was that, for the rest of the evening. It happened quite often recently.

The Doctor loaded his folding bicycle into the hoppicopter and visited the Rideouts. 'Peace!' he shouted, shattering the living-room peace. 'Tranquillity! Change and decay in all around I see – except here, in the bosom of the English home!'

'Your chauffeur girl, Polly . . . she isn't with you?' asked Mrs Rideout, hopefully.

'No, we have dismissed each other. I am not sad, her sniffing was becoming unbearable. Now she is to be a pop star. I have arranged it all.'

'What went wrong that evening on TV?' Mr Rideout asked.

'Ah, that is more interesting. *Most* interesting. Havoc in the basement! Cables, wiring, all that electronic knitting – damaged, destroyed, mutilated!'

'Blobs,' said Lucas, knowingly.

'No, that is the strange thing! Not blobs. Something as bad, even worse –'

But then Lettice came in – she had been avoiding the Doctor – and he said no more. Indeed, he quietened immediately when she entered. Quiet, he was at his best. To Lucas, he seemed to treat Lettice as if she were recovering from an illness. Gradually she warmed to him, even talked with him.

'Ah, the animals,' he said to her. 'Yes, it is all very strange and becoming stranger. A new phase, I think. Can animals be evil, Lettice?'

'Of course not! They just do what they're born to do . . . I mean, it's ridiculous to hate snakes and that sort of thing, they're not *evil* –'

'I do hope you are right, Lettice,' said the Doctor. 'I do so hope you are right.'

The Animals' Revolt

'All right, then!' said Mr Rideout, pulling on his gumboots. 'Everybody out! Sons of the soil! Daughters too, Lettice. And kindly don't clodhop all over the ground I've just dug. That's a *fine tilth* you're trampling on.'

Lettice picked up a garden fork and vaguely put it down again. She hated gardening.

'A fine tilth,' said Mr Rideout, happily. 'That's what's needed. Aerate the soil. Organic matter. Minerals, trace elements.' He began to sing: ' "We plough the fields and sca-a-tter, the good seed o'er the la-a-and . . ." '

Lucas took up the song: 'It really doesn't ma-a-tter, I'd rather buy things ca-a-nned!'

'It does matter,' said Mr Rideout. 'And you can't buy things canned.'

'You can,' said Lettice. 'Mother got all sorts of tinned things last week –'

'She won't get them much longer,' said Lucas. 'Everything's falling to pieces, everywhere. Our whole civilization's going up the creek. Bust. Finito.'

'We'll look back,' said Mr Rideout, 'and remember tinned ham and newspaper deliveries, and petrol, and battery eggs, and rashers of bacon and roast beef – we'll look back at these things and we'll *marvel*. Marvel! When you two have children of your own – that is, if the Blobs let you – they'll cluster round your knee and lisp, "Did you really eat *meat*, Mummy?

And Daddy, what were pork chops like?'' And you'll look down at the little eager, upturned faces, and you'll remember Yorkshire pudding and roast beef and gravy and you'll reply, "Belt up, you little morons!'' and burst into tears of self-pity and nostalgia. And then you'll go out into the garden, and pick up your nasty gardening tools, and dig and rake and hoe and weed. Just as we're going to do.'

They shouldered their tools, walked down the garden and started work. Mr Rideout continued digging up a corner of the lawn, soon to be a vegetable patch. Lucas worked with him, picking up the turves on a fork, banging the soil out and carting them away to the compost heap. Lettice gawkily prodded at the vegetable bed they had prepared the day before.

'You really do think,' said Lucas, 'that we'll never see meat again? I mean, eat it regularly?'

'Never!' his father said. 'Well, hardly ever. God, my back's killing me already!' He straightened up, glad of an excuse to stop work and deliver a lecture. 'How can you have meat if the animals refuse to stay in their fields, or go to the slaughterhouse? How can you have beef if the cattle try to kill the man holding the humane killer? And even assuming you can breed the animals, and raise them, and slaughter them for meat, how can you get the meat to market when the railways won't work and the lorries can't use the roads?' He started digging again, but soon stopped. 'You read that newspaper story about the lorries in France, didn't you? And the same sort of story about the cattle on the motorway?'

'I read them,' said Lucas. 'Here, let's swop. I'll dig and you do my job for a while.'

As Lucas dug, he thought about the French disaster. The newspapers and television had been full of it. During the night, on one of the major motorway routes, Blobs had appeared. Suddenly the road was blocked. Drivers of the great *camions*, the long-distance lorries, had been forced to slam on the brakes. There had been a few pile-ups. Some cars and light vehicles were able to work through, but the big lorries had to wait. More Blobs – and the queue built up: at first, for a few kilometres, then for fifty, and at last endlessly. No vehicle moved.

When day came, the drivers got out of their cabs and argued and shrugged. White-helmeted motorcycle police blew whistles and waved arms. The engines of the great lorries were started and the front of the queue moved forward.

But then the animals came. Mild-eyed, wet-nosed cows solemnly trampled hedges and fences and ambled along the roads. They looked innocent and silly. Occasionally a cluster of cows formed round a lorry and butted against it, slowly and regularly. The panelling was left bruised and dented: no real damage was done.

But sometimes, a driver who thought he knew about animals was trapped by the cows – pressed against the metal of his lorry by a shoving mass of heavy bodies and hard horns: when this happened, there was a cry from the trapped man – more cries from the men who came running to help him – the thrashing of sticks against unyielding bodies – and at last, the amiable herd of cows would move on, leaving a silent knot of humans standing round a crushed, silent, misshapen body.

The pigs were worse. There was a horrible intelligence and determination about the pigs. When the cows came, the lorry drivers grabbed sticks or jack handles and, half humorously, smacked and thwacked at the animals, expecting to drive them away. But when a horde of pigs burst through a hedge, their heads lowered and their mouths slavering and their long, fleshy bodies packed solid and coming fast, the drivers leaped into their cabs and slammed the doors.

The cabs of these great lorries were a long way from the ground. All the same, the pigs would reach up, standing on their hind legs and probing upwards with their dripping snouts. Sometimes, the knot of pigs round a particular lorry was so dense that more pigs could climb over the heaving backs and scrabble at a window or windscreen with their cleft feet. The drivers cursed, blew horns, even started the engine and rocked the lorry back and forth to shift the animals.

Generally this worked. Once or twice it failed. Windscreen glass shattered – the great body hurtled into the cab – the man's screams and the pig's screams became one – and then the man's voice was silent and from the cab came new, muffled sounds, slobberings and gruntings and gulpings. Outside the cab, there was a mounting crescendo of squeals as the whole heaving, thrusting mass of pigs tried to climb over itself to join the feast.

Yet even this was not all. Rats scurried over the tops of lorries. The little field animals, usually never seen, were everywhere. The TV cameras picked up a worried looking old horse, rolling its eyes and tossing its head, trotting aimlessly up and down the line, stumbling sometimes on little furry bodies. The horse did this for half a day, ever faster and more anxiously, then, when a Blob emerged from nothing in front of it, the horse dropped dead.

There were dogs barking at nothing – more dogs, forming groups that attacked the cows and pigs – still more dogs forming great packs that patrolled the lorry lines, or suddenly streamed off across country to attack people in villages and towns.

The French story was, so far, the worst of many. In England, the Blobs and the animals had seriously interrupted not only the production but also the distribution of food. Farms were in chaos, trains were derailed and motorways closed. There was a twenty-five mile queue on the Luton stretch of the M 1. At the airport nearby, an airliner crashed on take-off – a Blob appeared on the runway. The Dover ports and roads had been paralysed for three days and there seemed very little hope of sorting out the confusion.

In America, beef cattle were quite simply refusing to be killed. Blobs made the vast herds of animals hysterical. They burst out of the stockyards. Steers roamed the streets of Omaha. While throughout Europe, and in Asia, and Russia and –

'I thought you said you'd do the digging,' said Mr Rideout.

Lucas stopped thinking and started working. 'I don't know why you want the beans here,' he said. 'I mean, beans grow almost anywhere, don't they? This is good soil, why don't we save it for the tricky crops?'

'I don't give a damn what we do,' said Mr Rideout, suddenly angry, 'so long as we get the blasted seeds in the ground. Any crop, I don't care. Just let's get the ground *dug* and the seeds *planted*. You don't seem to realize – oh well, perhaps you do, but lots of people don't. You know there's already a shortage of seeds?'

'And a shortage of gardens. I wonder how people without gardens will get on.'

'Perhaps,' said Mr Rideout, 'they simply won't get on at all. And perhaps we'll be mounting guard over the cabbage patch a few months from now. Night-long vegetable vigil. Imagine that.'

Lucas imagined it: and dug.

That night, horses from the nearby riding stables broke loose. They blundered about in the Rideouts' garden, trampling flat the newly dug and planted ground, knocking over the toolshed, breaking fences.

Next morning, Lucas and his father surveyed the damage. 'I don't suppose it matters,' said Mr Rideout. 'And if it does, to hell with it. My back's a disaster area. I just can't face starting all over again.'

'Look at those rats!' said Lucas. There were half a dozen of them, poking their noses in the dents made by the horses' hooves. Sometimes a rat found a seed and ate it. After a time, the rats got bored. They moved away when stones were thrown at them.

'Rats!' said Mr Rideout. 'Coming out into the open like that! In broad daylight! Bet you never see a sight like that again!'

Next day, the rats came not in half-dozens, but in hundreds and thousands.

The rats were the beginning of the end.

The Rats

There can be no creature on earth more efficient than a rat. Before the Blobs came, the efficiency of rats – the unceasing rapidity of their breeding, their ability to thrive on almost any diet, their countless ways of making a living – had mattered very little to mankind. As far as man was concerned, rats were ugly, dangerous animals; eaters of filth, breeders of plagues and carriers of disease. But for most people, unpleasant as they were, rats had one virtue: you seldom saw them. You seldom if ever had a rat 'experience'. You shuddered when you read that rats in such-and-such a town had run wild and were pouring through the streets like a dirty river. You wondered at reports on the failure of the latest, most vicious poisons – apparently the rats had grown used to them, even grown to like them, so what could mankind do next? But you yourself seldom *saw* rats, because rats knew their place. You did not wish to meet rats; the rats did not wish to meet you. So the two societies – rats and men – lived apart.

The Blobs brought them together.

Suddenly, the rats left their hidden places and came out into the open. They erupted from the ground like lava from a volcano. They invaded.

As rats outnumber humankind by nobody-knows-how-many hundreds or thousands to one, the rat invasion was, from the first moment, irresistible. There could be no question of failure.

The behaviour of the rats themselves showed the certainty of their success. If a man faces a bison, or a lion, or a bear – and if the man stands his ground, or better still raises a rifle – the animal will, most probably, pause, turn and go. If you torment an animal much stronger and more powerful than yourself – an elephant, a horse, an ox – most probably you will get away with it. Even tigers can be taught to jump through hoops.

But nobody was going to tame the rats.

The day the rats came, Lettice saw the news on television. The news was about rats, rats, nothing but rats: a whole world of rats. Earlier, she had watched the rats in the garden. She had seen them eat her guinea-pigs, overturn the dustbins, form heaving knots and rings of grey bodies fringed with writhing, naked tails. Nobody had dared leave the house, for only in the house could you feel safe. Sickened and silent, Lettice made her way upstairs to the safety and isolation of her bedroom. She would go to bed and stay there.

She opened the bedroom door, unzipped her dress and screamed.

There were rats on her bed, three of them. They were eating a piece of chocolate she had put on her bedside table. One rat was sitting up like a squirrel, its yellow-brown teeth industriously nibbling through the paper wrapper and the silver paper beneath.

Lettice kept screaming. Lucas was the first to reach her. He saw the rats and felt a great bubble of nausea inside his chest. The sickness turned to a sort of trembling hate. He took his shoes off and flung them, one after the other, at the rats.

The first shoe missed and sent the bedside table lamp smashing across the room. With his other shoe, he hit a rat so hard that it was knocked off the bed. It squeaked loudly when it was hit and fell to the other side of the bed.

Lettice still screamed and Lucas yelled curses while he looked for something else to attack the rats with. He picked up Lettice's hockey stick, seized it and went towards the two rats still on the bed.

With unwinking red eyes, they watched him come. Their backs were humped. Their long naked tails twitched. The rat holding the chocolate did not drop it.

'Get *out*!' shouted Lucas. Or tried to shout: his voice would not work properly. He knew why. He was afraid – afraid of the two rats on the bed, terrified of the third rat that he could not see. Where was it?

Lettice was gone now. He heard her run down the stairs, screaming and sobbing, and his parents' voices. He wished his father would come upstairs. Where was the third rat? He was too frightened to approach the bed while the third rat could not be seen. He knew how rats attacked: the sudden darting run, the bunched, coil-sprung leap, the snap of the two long, fang-like front teeth ... he had plenty of time to learn about their habits during the day. Particularly when they had got to the guinea-pigs.

Where was the third rat?

There! By the edge of the bed! Despite himself, Lucas let out a yelp of fear and backed away, terrified of the sudden spring and the fastening of the hideous teeth in his ankle.

But the rat had nothing of the sort in mind. It looked at Lucas for a long moment, then scrambled busily up the bedspread to join the other two. It reached out its obscene front paws for the chocolate bar, snatched it away and started to nibble and crunch, tearing at the wrapping.

When its mouth was full, it paused. All three rats stared straight at Lucas. Lucas felt his face reddening. His first thought was that he was embarrassed – embarrassed, if you please! – by the staring eyes. His second thought was, 'I am ashamed. Ashamed of being afraid. But I *am* afraid, sick afraid . . .'

These thoughts took only split seconds – and then his father was in the room, pushing past him and gasping, 'Get out of the way, I'll *kill* – I'll *kill* –' He was carrying a few yards of nylon garden netting, strong, light stuff. He opened out the net and threw it over the rats. Immediately they began to scream and fight and scramble. Mr Rideout gathered the net together until he was holding a dangling bundle that writhed and heaved and squeaked and gibbered and thrust out jerking grey-pink limbs.

He clattered down the stairs, Lucas after him, making for the kitchen back door. 'In the garden,' he muttered. 'Kill them outside.'

His wife stopped him. 'Don't open the door! You'll let more of them in!'

'Boiler room,' said Mr Rideout and opened the little door leading from the kitchen. Lucas made to follow him into the small, bare room but his father said, 'Keep out! Out!'

So they kept outside and listened to the swinging thumps. At first there were squeaks and screams as well. But long after these were over, the swinging thumps went on.

When he came out, Mr Rideout's face was pasty and sweating and his nostrils were white. He was trembling and panting so much that he could barely speak. 'Filth!' he said. 'Filth! And the whole place could be full of them . . . Lucas, get me a whisky and make it a big one. Filth . . .!'

There was a pause while Mr Rideout washed his hands, then washed them again, in the kitchen sink. Lucas came in and said, 'I'm sorry, Dad, you're out of whisky, there's only sherry. I'm sorry . . .'

His father looked at him furiously, but as he looked his eyes became sane again. 'It was a good idea of mine, that netting,' he said, drinking the sherry. He went to the window and looked out into the darkness. By the dustbins, there was scuffling and squeaking and the noise of a lid rolling about as the rats scampered over it.

'A good idea,' he said. 'But, not good enough. There isn't that much netting in the whole wide world . . .'

The next day, Catchmouse was not there. Lettice was the first to notice. She called from the kitchen window – 'Catchy! Catchy!' – but there was no chirruping mew or sudden scurry of paws, followed by a plunge of the furry head into the food bowl.

Nobody said anything, not even Lettice. Everyone assumed – everyone but Lettice – that the rats had killed Catchmouse.

But Lettice had 'talked' with Catchmouse. She thought differently. She did not speak her thoughts.

Miss Ann Langham sat in the Rideouts' living-room with her legs – one ankle strapped – neatly crossed and her elegant hands folded in her lap. She made a picture of repose, relaxation and control. The picture was completely false. Without moving a muscle, she yet managed to radiate an almost hysterical tension.

The family pretended not to notice it. Mrs Rideout knitted, Mr Rideout fiddled with an unreliable pocket electronic calculator he had bought cheaply, Lettice stared at nothing and Lucas wiped oil over a Mark III Webley air rifle.

Mr Rideout had bought the air rifle second-hand many years ago for plinking at targets in the garden. Tiring of it – the Webley was so accurate that you could hardly miss – he had smeared it with Vaseline, wrapped it in brown paper and put it in the loft.

Now the rats had come, the air rifle was part of the Rideouts' life pattern.

Miss Langham had arrived earlier in the evening. She had been an increasingly frequent visitor to the Rideouts' since her flat-mate Josie, made hysterical by the rats, had left for Scotland. In the small country town where her parents lived, things were better.

This particular evening, the sound of the front-door bell ringing had started off the usual rat routine: Mr Rideout, hearing the bell, shouted 'Blast! – oh, all right,' went upstairs and poked the air rifle and his head out of his study window. 'Oh, it's you, Ann. Just coming. Keep moving.' The family heard Ann Langham making beating noises with a walking stick while she waited to be let in. Lucas went to the front door – waited for the shouted 'O K!' from his father – opened the door and hurried Miss Langham inside.

Nowadays, this was normal procedure, because of the rats.

Mrs Rideout said, 'Oh, hello Ann, it's you . . .' Ann replied by staring through Mrs Rideout; opening her still slightly scarred mouth; giving a single, sobbing scream; and falling forward in a faint. Luckily, Mrs Rideout broke her fall.

When Ann recovered, she told the Rideouts what had happened. Going back to her flat after the day's teaching, she had gone to the bathroom and found the lid of the w.c. at an odd angle, neither open nor closed. So she lifted the lid – to reveal a rat draped over the seat. It had eaten a poison that made it crave water.

'Unfortunately,' Ann said, 'I thought it was dead, but it wasn't. I got the dustpan and brush and when I'd scooped it into the dustpan it woke up and tried to bite me. But it couldn't move very fast, and so it was more or less limping around the room after me, opening and closing its jaws and leaving a trail of – stuff – behind it . . . and I felt rather sick.'

Lucas exchanged glances with his father, who said, 'Well, yes. You would.'

Ann said, 'I really felt unable to stay in the flat so I decided to come here. So I put my coat on again and went to pick up my handbag. And when I picked it up, it felt heavy, so I looked inside – and there was *another* rat, eating the lining or something –'

She shuddered and started to cry. Mr Rideout said, 'Well, that's rats for you, they'll eat anything,' and nodded his head violently at the cupboard where the drinks were kept. Lucas got Ann a drink and she began to recover. Now she sat tidily, like a well-disciplined nightmare.

The front-door bell sounded again and Mr Rideout said, 'Blast! – your turn, Lucas.' Lucas went upstairs with the rifle and eventually the new visitor was admitted. This time it was Doctor Kalabza, with a moped.

'I am come!' he announced. 'And how do you think I came? By pedal and mo! By moped! Despite the rats! Gumboots, you see. My new chauffeur left me – how can there be loyalty in these times? – and so I must pedal and mo – but what is this, can it be my lovely Miss Langham, my dearest student!'

She smiled whitely at him. Her face was so changed that even the Doctor was quietened.

The Option

They sat and talked. They talked, inevitably, of the Blobs, of the animals, of the breakdown of everyday life, and of the new horror, the plague of rats.

'What,' said Mrs Rideout, 'are we to *do*? What *can* we do? People won't go to work – can you blame them? The lorries and trains are stopping, the food shops are staying shut, the stuff we grow in the garden is eaten, our houses are infested, the electric cables are being bitten through, the old people are dying like flies . . . What can we do?'

For the first time, Lettice spoke. 'Opt out!' she said. 'Go! Leave! Pack up and get out!'

Everyone rounded on her. 'You *can't* opt out, it's the same all over the world!' 'Where would you pack up and go *to*?' 'Trust Lettice to come up with something absolutely *stupid* . . .!'

Lettice said, 'Catchmouse did and Duff's going to.'

'Going to *what*?'

'Emigrate!' said Lettice.

'Emigrate *where*? Emigrate *how*? Emigrate *when*?' shouted Lucas.

'Just emigrate!' said Lettice. 'It's obvious! Catchmouse has gone already, she told me. And Duff's going any time now, aren't you Duff? You're leaving us all and going, aren't you Duff? Even leaving me!' She cuddled Duff and buried her nose in his neck.

'What's she babbling on about?' said Lucas, disgustedly.

'Wait a minute, friend Lucas!' said Doctor Kalabza. 'Wait a very little minute! Let us hear more of this emigration, Lettice! Tell us everything about it!'

Lettice explained.

'I was talking to them both the other night,' she began. 'First Catchmouse – but she got in a huff and walked away – then Duff. They both said the same thing. As I keep telling you, Catchmouse has done it already. Being a cat, Catchy doesn't really care about us, not like darling Duff –'

'Never mind about lovey-dovey darling Duff,' said Lucas. 'Get on with it.'

'The rats got Catchy,' said Mr Rideout, gruffly. 'You know that, Lettice. We all know it. So don't start making up silly stories.'

'*Is* it a silly story, Lettice?' said the Doctor.

'I'm not making up a story. I'm just telling you a fact. Catchy's chosen to go.'

'Where?'

'Wherever it is they go,' Lettice said. 'To some other time, or some other place. I *know*.'

'How do you know, Lettice?' said the Doctor.

'Catchmouse told me,' said Lettice. She was getting pink and angry, but it was quite obvious that she was convinced of what she was saying. 'She sat on my chest in, you know, the usual way, and I was trying to find out what she thought about the rats. But it only made her angry, she bristled and stuck her claws in, you know. But I kept on at her, because I thought that she, being a cat, might know more about rats than we do. I thought she might have some sort of answer to them, I don't know. But she said there isn't any answer to rats. She went on and on about killing *a* rat and how she killed *single* rats. She was all bloodthirsty. But when I asked

her about dealing with *millions* of rats, she just got uneasy. But
I held on to her and made her concentrate and asked her
what *she* was going to do about it. And she told me what I've
told you: she was going to leave.'

'Another time or another place . . .' said Doctor Kalabza.
'Possibly . . .'

'I've tried to get in touch with her since she left,' Lettice
said. 'You know, you lie there and concentrate and concentrate, and after a time you think you may be getting some
response or contact or whatever it is – I've tried all that, but I
can't be sure. I think she was with me last night . . . I *think*
she was, but I don't really know, it could have been me,
making it up . . .'

'Assume that she *was* with you the other night,' said the
Doctor. 'What did she tell you? What did she say?'

'She simply said – or perhaps I only felt that she said – that
it's quite all right where she's gone to, the rats were just
ordinary rats, the way they used to be.' Lettice looked uncertain.

'Anything else?'

'Oh yes, there was another thing! She said she'd had fish
that day! I remember now, she kept on and on about the fish,
and how good it was! So perhaps I really was in touch with
her after all! It was a flaky white fish, like cod, I'm sure she
showed it to me with her mind! And it was boiled, it must
have been a leftover!'

'So . . .' said the Doctor. 'Catchmouse is gone. Gone on a
journey. Or so you tell us, dear Lettice. Lettice, this is most
important, so think carefully – you tell us that Duff is to go
very soon?'

'Yes, just like Catchy. When Catchy was with me on my
chest, she got all excited – I couldn't hold on to her mind, she
was too excited. So I got hold of Duff and made him talk to
me.

'He was just the same as Catchy about the rats. He doesn't mind one rat, he likes going for it, but he's as frightened as we are of *all* the rats. And in the end, he said he was going to do what Catchy had done (he knew all about it, they used to talk to each other quite a lot). He said he was going. But then he got all sentimental about leaving us and started being soppy.'

'In other words,' Lucas said, 'you don't really know if he is going or not. We can't check on him, so we can't know if what you say is true or not. I mean, if he stays, you simply say, "Well, I never said definitely that he was going!" and if the rats get him and he disappears, you'll say, "Ah! I always told you he'd go!" '

'That's not fair!' said Lettice, but the Doctor put his hand on her arm and said, 'It *is* fair, Lettice, so I want you to think very carefully and not get upset . . .

'Now, if Duff *does* go, will there be a certain time when he goes? Will he choose day or night? Morning or evening? I ask you this, dear Lettice, so that we may *observe* Duff and hope to *see* him go and thus discover the very important truth underlying what you believe. And what I believe too. But what I believe does not matter, I am out of my depth. Only you can tell us, Lettice. You are the great scientist now.'

'What do you want me to do?' she said.

'Suppose, Lettice, you had a talk with Duff. Suppose you said to him, "Duff, I think you should go. Go at a certain time." Then we could observe him, see him go. Do you see?'

'Yes, but he's such a silly old thing, and he's so fond of us. I mean, he might say he'd do it and then not do it.'

'Ah, but suppose you gave him a reason for doing it! Suppose you said to him, "Duff, you should go, it is quite all right for you to go. And what is more, my good dog, if *you* go, then *I* will go too!" '

'But I couldn't say that, it would be a lie!' said Lettice.

'Would it be a lie?' said the Doctor, sitting back in his chair and putting his little hands on his knees. 'Are you sure it would be a lie, Lettice?'

There was a long silence. At last, Lettice jumped to her feet and cried, 'You could be right! I never thought of it like that, Doctor Kalabza! – I mean, I'm so used to people laughing at me and thinking me a liar, that I half think myself a liar even when I know I'm telling the truth! I mean, just suppose we all *have* to go . . .! Come on, Duff!'

They heard her running up the stairs – opening her bedroom door – calling, 'Come on, Duff!' – slamming the door shut – then silence.

'Now, dear friends,' said Doctor Kalabza, 'we will continue to talk. But very quietly, so as not to disturb Lettice. Softly, then. Softly!'

Pin Money

'You can't go back through time,' said Mrs Rideout flatly. 'Man, woman, dog or cat, it simply can't be done. So I don't really see why you are taking Lettice seriously, Doctor.'

'Funny things do happen, though,' said Mr Rideout. 'That bloke who bent forks, on TV. Indian fakirs. There was a fakir – never saw him myself – who could turn his bowels inside out –'

'Really!' said Mrs Rideout.

'And perfect pitch, that's a remarkable thing. Hear a note, name it. Fairy rings. ESP, psycho-kinesis. And what was that thing on telly only the other night? –'

'Telly,' said Doctor Kalabza. 'Ah, television. People are so strange. Here you are, Mr Rideout, a reasonable, rational, scientifically minded man – yet you believe in television and radio waves!'

'Believe in them? Of course I believe them! I can see and hear them in action any time I choose!'

'But – let us talk softly, Mr Rideout, let us not disturb Lettice – you cannot produce them, show them to me, let me handle them. Perhaps the radio wave is all belief, Mr Rideout? Simply a bit of folk-lore that we act on?'

'You mean that if everyone stopped believing in radio and television the waves would die? Like the fairy Tinkerbell?

"Come on, children! All together, now! Do you believe in telly?"'!'

'Beliefs change, Mr Rideout. This generation believes in radio waves and *voilà*! – radio and television! But think back, dear Mr Rideout! Think back to witches and witchdoctors, ghosts and evil spirits, and the bell, book and candle!'

'Phooey,' said Mr Rideout. 'You have your witchcraft and I'll have my switchcraft!' He patted the TV set.

'Pins!' said Mrs Rideout. 'I've suddenly remembered. Witches used to vomit pins! It was their parlour trick. Just fancy vomiting *pins*, oh dear me!'

'Ah, but dear Mrs Rideout, do not laugh! You are forgetting your own English history! Disbelieving your own written records! Now, let me remind you: when witchcraft was prevalent in this country and when there was much gossip and constant gossip about the witches, you had a Judge Jeffreys. You know him?'

'The Bloody Assizes,' said Lucas. 'Judge Jeffreys used to tour the country trying witches – well, condemning them, anyhow. You could hardly call them trials –'

'You have read these trials, Lucas?'

'Yes, bits of them. History lessons.'

'Then you may know that there are many, many, many records and documents and evidences of women who, said to be witches, vomited pins. Vomited pins in the court rooms, before the eyes of judges and lawyers!

'Now, just consider for a moment, I beg you. Just think. Here is the stern judge in his wig. There is an old woman, said to be a witch. The judge, she knows, will condemn her to a horrible death: it does not matter what she says, innocent or guilty does not matter, for he is the Hanging Judge, Judge Jeffreys. She must surely die.

'So he says to this doomed old woman, "You are a wicked witch, do not deny it!" and she says, "Yes, I am, and I glory in it! It is good that I am a witch, and I put my witch's curse on you! And that you may know I am truly a witch, I vomit pins before your very eyes!" And she brings up the little glittering pins, and the people gasp, and the judge has her burned – and the recorder of the court writes it all down, my dear Rideouts; writes it all down so that centuries later, we may see that a professional man, a legal man, has seen a woman vomit pins . . .!

'And this,' the Doctor continued, 'at a time when pins were so expensive that the husband had to give his wife special money to buy them –'

' "Pin money",' said Lucas.

'Just so,' said the Doctor. ' "Pin money".'

'Well, I'm sure you know best,' said Mrs Rideout. 'But why pins, I simply don't know!'

'But surely you must see!' cried the Doctor. 'Pins, because – I must speak quietly, Lettice is at work – pins, because *pins were expected*! For the conjurer, a white rabbit: for the psychokinetics, the bending fork: for us, the electronic device, the TV set: for Christians, the crucifix: for witches, cats, broomsticks and *pins!*'

'It was the fish, originally,' said Mr Rideout. 'For Christians, I mean. The fish was their symbol. And the chi-rho. Then the sign of the cross. All very interesting, Doctor. Would you like a sherry?'

The Doctor rolled his eyes upwards and shrugged his shoulders. 'You do not seem to understand,' he said, coldly.

'I do!' said Lucas, flaming with a sudden excitement. 'At least, I think I do! What I mean is, that today, we live in an electronic age and we watch the TV and listen to the radio – and we take it all for granted, though we don't really *understand* – no, I mean, we can't actually *touch* and show someone the power that makes all the gadgets go . . . While in the old days, they had –'

'In the old days,' said Ann, as excited as Lucas, 'they built cathedrals more wonderful than any buildings we have today! – and vomited pins! – and there are still witchdoctors in some parts of the world! – and –'

'And because they believed these quite different things,' said the Doctor, 'and because so *many people* believed those things, those things could work. The witches *could* and *did* vomit pins! We *can* and *do* snatch music and pictures from the air for our magic boxes, our radios and televisions! The witchdoctors, the man who bends the spoons – surely you must see, dear people, it is all a matter of *belief*!

'Now, in this very house, at this very moment, we have a girl called Lettice. She believes she can talk to the animals; and she believes the animals believe they can travel in time or space. *And she could be right*!'

'She could be wrong,' said Mr Rideout. 'Here's your sherry.'

'She hasn't been proved wrong about the Blobs,' said Lucas. 'She hasn't been proved wrong about talking to animals.'

'I don't know,' said Ann, slowly. 'Suppose she's right about everything, I still don't see that it makes much difference. Pins, fakirs, radio waves, religions – they could all work because, as you said, Doctor, nearly all the people believed they could work. So there was a huge power of belief to draw on. Without that amount of power – *everyone* believing – what can Lettice, and a few more like her, achieve? Assuming, of course, that she *is* right. And I'm not sure yet about that.'

There were footsteps coming downstairs and Lettice came into the room followed by Duff.

'Duff's going on Tuesday,' she said. 'Before the dustmen come. You know how he hates the dustmen. So it will be Tuesday morning.'

Duff's Departure

On Tuesday morning, the road outside the Rideouts' house was jampacked. For once, the rats had to give way to the humans – and their vehicles, cameras, generators, cable runs, tripods, lighting gear . . .

The TV producer asked, for the third time, 'When did you say they'll come? The dustmen? What time?'

'I don't know,' replied Mrs Rideout, worriedly. 'Nothing works properly these days. They might not even come at all, how can I possibly *tell* –'

'Duff will leave before noon, whether they come or not,' said Lettice. Her face was set with determination. 'He expects them at noon and he'll go before noon. He told me so again, for the umpteenth time, last night.'

'Yes . . .' said the TV man, looking at Lettice with un-believing eyes. 'Yes, no doubt . . .'

He stared at Duff and other eyes followed his. There were perhaps two dozen people – journalists, photographers, elec-tricians, TV crewmen – crowded in the living-room. They were all there because Dr Kalabza had given them a news story, and a Dr Kalabza story had to be followed up. But not one pair of eyes showed any belief.

Which was hardly surprising. Duff, the star of the occasion, looked nothing like a star. He was stretched out on his familiar patch of rug, nose between front paws. His eyes were watery. Embarrassed by the staring humans, he looked up – found nothing to interest him – and began to scratch one floppy ear.

'I've always preferred cats,' said a cynical voice. A few people laughed.

Duff stopped scratching and turned his head, looking for Lettice. When he saw her, he got shakily to his feet and went to her. Although she was standing, he managed to lay his head in her lap. She patted his head and said, 'It's all right, Duff, really it is. Oh dear . . .'

The dog made a sound between a woof and a howl and Lettice began to cry. Some camera shutters clicked and you could hear tape recorders whirring.

'What's the time now, then?' said a photographer.

'Eleven-twenty. Not long to go. If we're going, that is.'

Duff went to Mrs Rideout and stared at her, mournfully. Again, cameras clicked. Uncertainly, Mrs Rideout said, 'Good dog, Duff. There's a good boy, then! Oh dear, *must* they walk all over the vegetable-bed? Mr – I don't know your name, but would you *kindly* tell your men *not* to –'

The men in the garden pretended to move their equipment away from the barren vegetable plot. Minutes went by. Duff stood in the middle of the people in the room, almost still. Sometimes he moved his head from side to side and sometimes he looked up at Lettice, who stood by him.

At last, he went to the rug and sniffed at his own particular place on it. 'Oh Gawd, he's going to settle down for a nice long sleep!' someone said.

He was wrong. Duff sniffed busily at the rug – turned again to Lettice – and made for the garden. The men and machines out there made room for the girl and the dog. Someone held a microphone in front of Lettice's mouth and asked her a question, but she did not seem to hear. Dr Kalabza, who had been giving interview after interview, said, 'Leave her alone, my friend, be a little kind. Soon, she and her dog will be apart.'

'Too sad,' said a girl reporter, nastily.

The Doctor ignored the sneer. He was watching Lettice and Duff. Down the road, there was the noise of a car coming or going. One of Duff's ears went up, then down again. You could almost see him say to himself, 'Not the dustmen.' His eyes were wetter than ever and his tail was on the ground. He gazed at Lettice, adoring her.

'Duff,' she said, 'I think it's time. I think you'd better go. Go, Duff.'

Heads were bent, cameras were focused, settings and levels were checked.

'Go on, Duff,' she said. 'It's all right for you to go now. Darling Duff . . .'

The dog walked his old shaky walk to the far corner of the lawn; stopped; looked back at Lettice; and –

– *vanished*.

Within hours, the world was told and shown what had happened.

Within days, the arguments were beginning to peter out. What was the point of arguing? There, again and again on the screen or in the newspapers and magazines, was the proof. One moment a dog: next moment, no dog. One moment, bored and sceptical faces: the next, faces fixed in open-mouthed astonishment . . . with only two exceptions. Dr Kalabza's face, intent and interested, showed no surprise; Lettice's face, tears on its cheeks, showed only grief.

Within weeks, new stories began to come in – new, but the same. There could be no doubt about it: the animals were leaving. There were too many stories, from too many parts of the globe, to permit doubt.

Humans were leaving too.

A very old and overdressed lady in a New York hotel loudly announced her determination to emigrate. The press and TV men turned up to watch her go. She went. She vanished.

A wild-haired, bead-covered leader of a crazy religious sect in Australia announced that he and all his followers were about to emigrate in a body, all at once. They did. They vanished.

It accelerated. A tribe of Africans, starving and drought-stricken, stood chanting on a hill-top with their arms outlifted. They stood like this for hours, until the weaker-willed dropped their arms. Then their leader gave a sudden screaming shout of command — everyone jumped at once — and the whole tribe seemed to spring into the sky and disappear. Even the weak ones vanished. It made fascinating TV.

Sane, respectable, bus-catching, ordinary, reliable, dull people announced that they would disappear: and did.

Doctor Kalabza was more than ever an international celebrity. Wherever he went (and he went everywhere) he trailed cameramen and reporters. His fame had never been so great. Yet now he no longer frolicked and clowned. Sometimes, he was almost grim.

Lettice was a high priestess, a goddess. She disliked it. She went around the house sulkily, complaining of the constant ringing and banging at the front door, the never-ending telephone calls, the stacks of letters in the hall. She looked, crossly, at the pictures of herself in the newspapers, muttering 'I don't look like that at *all*!' Then she would disappear for an hour or so and come downstairs with her hair done a new way. When Ann called, Lettice grabbed her and demanded an opinion about the new hairstyle.

Her chief complaint, the one she repeated all the time, was, 'If we're *going*, why don't we *go*? I promised Duff, you all know I promised him!'

'Oh, do shut up!' said Lucas. 'We can't go yet, it's obvious!'

'Why not, I'd like to know?'

'Well, we just *can't*, I mean, the world's still going on, we can't just leave.'

'Why not?'

'Well, we can't go unless everyone goes . . . we can't just go on our own, as a family, it wouldn't be . . .'

'Wouldn't be what?'

He didn't really know what or why. Nobody did. They stayed on because – because why? Because emigration was not absolutely, completely, universally certain? Because you cannot just leave behind a whole lifetime of familiar houses and faces and work? Because no one knew what to expect when they found themselves in the Other Place or the Other Time?

The last reason was probably the real reason. There were too many mysteries to face. To find answers to the mysteries, the world asked Lettice (and a thousand fakes and false prophets who pretended to have her powers) for an answer. 'What is it like Over There? Should we go? Can we go? Is it . . . all right?' Mainly through the agency of Doctor Kalabza, she tried to give answers.

Sometimes she answered the questions in person. More than once, she gave in to the throngs of people at the front door and appeared on television, looking much prettier than she had ever looked in the old days, but still nervous and uncertain.

'You've got to understand,' she said weakly to the cameras and microphones, 'I'm not a *scientist* or anything like that, I only know what the animals tell me – I mean, *used* to tell me in the old days. Catchmouse? No, I never get anything from Catchy, I suppose she's just settled down, the way cats do. What does Duff say? Well, he doesn't *say* much, he's just lonely for me and the family, he just goes on about personal things . . . like, when am I coming . . .'

Whatever she said, and however weakly and uncertainly she said it, the results were always the same: huge headlines in next day's popular papers. If, picking nervously at her lip, she said, 'Well, I really don't know,' the headlines howled 'LETTICE'S LIPS ARE SEALED! NO NEW REVELATIONS FROM WONDER GIRL'. If she said, 'It's poor old Duff I'm worried about,' the headlines yelled 'MY AGONY'. If she said, 'I suppose we'll go eventually,' the headlines thundered 'WILL LITTLE LETTICE MAKE HER BID FOR FREEDOM?'

Reading these headlines, Doctor Kalabza roared with laughter, Lucas chortled, Mr Rideout snorted, Mrs Rideout looked dimly pleased. And Lettice turned various colours and gave despairing howls.

And the world at large believed what was said. Not the words, but the feeling – the feeling of excitement, drama, possibility and hope.

Rampage

The rats became bolder and the Blobs suddenly became worse than ever.

Perhaps it was the never-ending television viewing that stirred up the Blobs. Everyone turned on their sets to learn the latest news about the rats, the emigrants, the latest shortages and disasters – and Lettice. So the Blobs, stung by the effects of Raster, went on the rampage.

It became so bad that the Common Market countries put forward a scheme to cut out television entirely, for a trial period of a week. The Americans and Russians considered the plan. Doctor Kalabza made yet another TV appearance and supported it.

So, in nearly all those countries where TV was most used, suddenly the screens went blank. Immediately, the Blobs seemed to quieten down.

But then the week was up, and the TV programmes started again.

On the very first day, the Blobs attacked with a viciousness worse than anything before. In the streets of New York, cars seemed to heave and shudder – then topple sideways, pushed over by the rampaging Blobs. In Paris, old buildings swayed and toppled, crushing passers-by and the people inside. In London, the Northern, Central and Circle underground lines were completely stopped – the Blobs were on the tracks. Before it was cut off, the electricity burned them. A new and horrible smell wafted up the lift and elevator shafts and sickened the people in the streets.

From Berlin and Amsterdam, Brussels and Geneva, Brasilia and Corfu, the reports poured in. The Blobs had made their way to the top of a big store – the floor had given way – the Blobs tumbled and smashed their way down, floor by floor, and lay in the basement, crushing the dying and wounded humans. The Blobs flattened cowsheds, air terminals, cottages, hotels.

The Blobs had become dedicated killers: and the rats, scurrying over the dead, found what they were looking for, ate it and grew fat.

As if it were a family fallen on hard times, the human race slowly came to realize the horrible truth. The old home had to be quitted; the old ways were, from now on, just happy memories; a new, uncertain and unpleasant future had to be faced.

'The Baxter boy's gone,' reported Ann one day. Now she lived with the Rideouts. 'I don't know how his parents will manage. Mrs Baxter's arthritis . . .'

'I didn't think he'd go,' said Lucas. 'He'd only just got that Honda from that bloke who emigrated. He was crazy about it.'

'Well, that girl-friend of his left. And Mrs Baxter says, when Barry read her goodbye letter, he just went straight out to the motorbike without a word –'

'Final burn-up to relieve his feelings?' said Lucas.

'Yes, just that. But when he got to the bike it was lying on its side. The Blobs, I suppose. He got it back on its stand, but some electric wires had been eaten through by rats. So he went back into the house and said, "Sorry, Mum, sorry Dad, but I've had it. I'm off." And he went.'

'Have the Baxters told Relief Patrol?'

'Yes, I saw to that. The Patrol people have been round already. Seen to the dustbins, brought in some food, blocked up holes where the rats could get in, and all the usual things. But of course, the Baxters can't carry on . . . she says they're leaving. Mr Baxter doesn't want to –'

'He's bone idle, that man,' said Mrs Rideout. 'He never does *anything*. Do you think they'll go?'

'Yes. Probably today.'

'Should we say goodbye, or anything?' said Mrs Rideout. 'No, I don't suppose so,' she answered herself. 'We never really *knew* them. And besides . . .'

'And besides, we'll be going ourselves!' said Lucas. 'All I want to know is, *when*!'

Conversations of this sort took place all over the world.

At first, people had said, 'We might.'

Later, they said, 'We could.'

Recently, they said, 'We will.'

Nowadays, the only question left was, '*When*?'

The Rideouts had not yet found it possible to answer the question.

Mr Rideout didn't want to go. Nor did Mrs Rideout. Both were old enough to fear change – yet feared the changes taking place every day as the rats and the Blobs took over their world, their country, their village and their home. Mr Rideout was worried because his money was going fast and he could earn no more: yet money was no longer needed. You got what you could when the government vans called; bought whatever the shops still had to sell. Perhaps what really worried him was that his occupation was gone. 'I was always a luxury,' he said. 'A parasite. A *scribbler*. And now there's no place left for me.'

'So we're going?' said Lucas.

'Ah,' said Mr Rideout, 'I didn't say *that* . . . I wonder if that new typing paper has come? I'll cycle down to the village and find out. Where's the Webley?'

He came back in triumph with a ream of typing paper. 'Look at that!' he cried. 'Last the world will ever see! – or that's the impression they gave me in the shop. Clean, white, virgin paper! The very essence of civilization! The raw material of all the most worthwhile things achieved by humanity!' He chuckled and took the package upstairs to his room. The family heard the typewriter going.

'Well,' said Mrs Rideout, 'I'm glad he's happy for an hour or two. But I can't really see what a difference it makes, his clean white paper.'

'He'll run out of steam soon,' Lucas said. 'Then we can use the paper in the loo. It's flimsy stuff, I could tell by the thickness of the package.'

Next day, however, Mr Rideout thumped downstairs in fury, holding a sheet of tattered typing paper with a corner missing. 'Look at it!' he shouted. 'Just look at it! Eaten by rats! They've spoiled the lot! – gone right through the whole pile!'

Emigration moved one step nearer for the Rideouts.

Days passed.

Now there were only five houses occupied in the Rideouts' street. Mrs Clavering would never leave. She was eighty. 'I've had my life,' she said, 'and it's been a good one. The Patrol people are very kind. Oh yes, I've had my life and don't regret a minute of it. So what have I to worry about?'

The Patrol people found what the rats left of her two days later.

That left four houses with people in them.

Doctor Kalabza arrived. He came in a car he had picked up. His Lagonda could not be reached: its garage was flooded by a sea of rats. But there were abandoned cars everywhere, many with keys in the ignition and petrol in the tank. You just took one and ran it until the tank was dry. Lucas had already 'owned' four cars. It was not safe to walk, of course, because of the rats. But it was not safe to drive either because of the Blobs.

Doctor Kalabza's car was a Lotus, very low and sporty. They could hear its gears clashing long before he arrived. He was clean-shaven but the rest of him – his clothes and even the whites of his eyes – was dirty.

'Dear people!' he cried. 'Still here! But that is a mistake, a terrible mistake! I have been thinking of you so much, in all the many places I have been! in Tokyo, Dublin, Los Angeles – in all the places, I think of you! But why are you still here, how do you exist?'

'I've been waiting for the Rideouts to go,' laughed Ann, 'and they've been waiting for me!'

'But that is so ridiculous!' said the Doctor. 'Why do you not go? For me it is different, I wish to observe unto the very last – but for *you* to stay, what purpose can there be?'

'You used to say,' Lucas said bitterly, ' "Leave it all to me! I'll find a way!" '

'Oh, but I was always a fool,' said the Doctor, lightly. 'A wise fool. And I am still a fool and that is why I am still here. But you, you must go!'

Lettice had said nothing. Now she spoke.

'We are going,' she announced flatly. 'Tonight. I promised Duff and I broke my promise, but now I'm going to keep it. Tonight.'

'Lettice!' cried Mrs Rideout, scandalized.

'Tonight, Mother,' said Lettice. 'With or without. I've spoken to Duff and he says it's all right where he is.'

'Spoken to Duff?' said the Doctor.

'Yes. Well, I think so. You can't really tell. But if we *did* talk, it sounds much better over there than it is here.'

'But dear child, what did he tell you?' said the Doctor.

'All sorts of things. More than ever before. I got sort of pictures of the people and places . . . I don't know if they're true or not, the pictures show what a dog sees, not what we see –'

'Past or future, dear Lettice?' said the Doctor, urgently. 'Tell me – Do we seem to travel backwards in time or forwards?'

'It seems to be backwards,' said Lettice. 'Women in long skirts and men wearing tall hats. Dark clothes. And there are horses everywhere.'

Mr Rideout snorted. 'Impossible!' he said. 'All this talk of moving forward in time, or backwards – a logical impossibility. You can't go to the past. The past has already happened and you can't make it re-happen. And even if you could, you'd go through a cycle of history that would bring you once again to the present –'

'Please, please, let us hear Lettice,' Doctor Kalabza insisted. 'At least she speaks from experience.'

'Oh no she doesn't,' said Mr Rideout, beginning to lose his temper. 'She speaks through the mind of a stupid old dog who may or may not be in touch with her. Look, Doctor: travelling backwards in time is a particularly pointless exercise in impossibility. Logically, it ends up with someone trying to put on his slippers and finding he's already in them. Surely you can see –'

'Mr Rideout, Mr Rideout, I see very clearly! By objecting to impossibilities, you make yourself sound as I sounded, poor foolish Doctor Kalabza, only a few weeks ago. Blobs are impossible, you say? But there are Blobs. They cannot come into our world and try to share it? But they have done so, they do so. It is impossible to talk to animals? Your daughter proves that she has done so. We cannot move ourselves to another dimension or time? Thousands of people do it every day.'

'Not to the past,' said Mr Rideout, stubbornly.

'I never said the past. It is you who keeps insisting on that. I asked Lettice, "Do we *seem* to travel backwards?" –'

'You should say what you mean,' said Mr Rideout, red with temper. 'Just what *do* you mean?'

'Backwards, forwards – I agree that such travelling may well be a logical and physical impossibility. But Mr Rideout, has it not occurred to you that we may be able to travel *sideways*?'

'*Sideways*?' said Mr Rideout contemptuously.

'Sideways! We may be able to move to parallel lives, lived along parallel lines.'

Lucas said, 'I know one thing about parallel lines: they never meet.'

'That was before Einstein,' his father grumbled. 'Nowadays, parallel lines behave like courting couples, apparently. Always cuddling up to each other . . .' He was growing tired of the argument. But the Doctor was not to be stopped.

'Parallel lines, parallel lives!' he exclaimed. 'Surely you can see it? Was there another Shakespeare, identical to your Shakespeare, except that he was a busy French farmer who never had time to write plays? –'

'Or a Burmese Bugs Bunny who hates carrots,' grumbled Mr Rideout.

The Doctor did not hear him. 'In this parallel world, must television be invented and accepted? Perhaps not! And then, without television, would the Blobs be content to stay in their own parallel world? Very probably!'

As if the word 'Blobs' had been a magician's 'Abracadabra', the whole house shook. The ceiling began to collapse. Everyone ran to the bay window. In the garden, they could see

Blobs. There was a herd of them, flickering and wavering and heaving. They pushed their great crisscrossed flanks against the walls of the house. More of the ceiling fell.

Some of the herd seemed to concentrate on what they were doing. These creatures stopped, turned and butted themselves against the kitchen wall. There was an appalling, long-drawn, smashing, tinkling, clattering, thundering uproar as the kitchen and everything in it was smashed.

The Blobs lost interest and moved on.

Doctor Kalabza, Ann and the Rideouts brushed the plaster dust off their hair and clothes. Ann said, 'I'm going,' and left. More plaster fell from the ceiling. 'In the garden, everyone,' Mr Rideout said. 'Safer out there.'

Outside, he said, 'Show of hands. Family decision. Go now, or later?' His voice was very grim. Hands were raised. Mrs Rideout's hand went up last. She was crying, silently.

'Unanimous,' Mr Rideout said. 'We go. Very well. We'll drink a toast to the future, if there is a future. I've got a bottle of champagne somewhere, I know I have.'

'The Blobs have broken all the glasses,' Mrs Rideout said, through her tears.

'Then we'll have to pass the bottle round. If I can find it.' He stumped off.

'And you,' Lettice said to the Doctor, 'what about you? Are you coming with us?'

'My dear Lettice, I wish I were. I am sure it will be most exciting. And of course you are right to go, you must go. Everyone should go.'

'Then why didn't you raise your hand?'

'Ah, well,' he began. She stared at him. He had run out of words – something she had never seen him do before. 'Ah, well, I am not family. And in any case, it would be difficult for me to go. Almost a matter of loyalty . . .'

'*Loyalty*? Loyalty to what?'

'To my science,' he replied. 'You will laugh at me, dear Lettice – laugh at me and my old-fashioned, out-dated science –'

'I'm not laughing! How could I laugh? But I don't understand.'

'Oh, I'm sure you do. It is simple. My science, the old science, is very simple. You look at things and try to see how they work – try to *see*, with a telescope, a microscope, an X-ray. So many ways to see, so many things to be seen –'

'Come with us,' she muttered.

'But then,' he said, ignoring her, 'there comes along something completely new, something that cannot be seen; only felt and known. By a new sort of scientist. You, Lettice! The new scientist for the new science.'

'That's silly,' she said. 'Please come with us. Please.'

Lucas joined them. 'You'll be killed if you don't,' he said, in a very low voice.

'I must stay,' said Doctor Kalabza. 'I must be here to see the end. I must live it, record it, make a record, a sort of tablet of stone –'

'A gravestone,' Lucas said. '*Your* gravestone.'

'No, dear Lucas – a stone for the whole world. I must inscribe it carefully, scientifically, faithfully. It must be a thing of – of –'

'Dignity?' Lettice said, softly. She could not see the Doctor's face, her eyes were full of tears. But Lucas could see it clearly. It was all there in the Doctor's eyes – the fearlessness, the dedication, the thrust of raw intelligence. And the fear.

'Found it!' cried Mr Rideout, flourishing a bottle of champagne. 'The rats have been at the cork but no harm done. Hope the wire broke their teeth. Here we go, then!'

The cork popped, the wine frothed. 'You first, my dear,' Mr Rideout told his wife. 'Take a good swig, don't just sip at it! Then pass it round.'

The Rideouts drank, avoiding looking at the familiar sights all round them – the trampled garden, the roofs of the deserted neighbouring houses, the gnawed posts of the old garden swing, the green watering can under the always-dripping tap. They drank and tasted nothing.

They put on layer after layer of clothing. If there was weather in the new place, it might be bad. If there was a new place.

'Well, Doctor,' Mr Rideout said, with an awful heartiness.

'Go!' he replied.

They went.

On the Other Side

It was an overcrowded room, rather too hot, filled with knick-knacks and framed photographs, potted plants and china figurines, glaring mirrors and dark wallpaper, carpets and rugs, doilies and trinkets. A Victorian family would have been quite at home in it.

Mr Rideout sat in the largest of the elaborately carved and padded chairs. His feet, in slippers decorated by his wife's careful needlework, rested on the brass surround. He was half-reading the local newspaper he owned and edited; but was constantly distracted by Lettice's piano practice. Her touch was lumpish and her sense of time and tone uncertain. As note followed note, each exactly wrong, his free hand fidgeted with the watch chain across his waistcoat. He wished himself elsewhere – preferably at the public house down the road – but could feel his wife's eyes glancing at him, imprisoning him within the family circle. He frowned and stuck out his lower lip.

Mrs Rideout, too, found the piano's noise irksome. There was a slight jerkiness to her hands as they drew the coloured threads through her tambour. Nonetheless, her brow remained serene beneath the centrally parted wings of shining hair drawn back from her brow. In that other world, her hair had been loosely dressed in careless waves. In this parallel world, she looked a different being: tauter, harder, more determined.

'That will suffice, Lettice,' she said. Lettice, relieved, stopped playing instantly. Duff, by the fireside, gave a long wheeze and settled his nose on his paws. Now he could sleep, undisturbed by the din from the big black noise-box. Catchmouse, sleeping, stopped flicking one ear and settled into a still more luxurious position.

'I wish I did not have to continue with my piano lessons, Mama,' said Lettice.

'So do we all,' said Lucas, saucily, not looking up from the pile of stereoscopic photographs at his knee. They were all familiar to him and boring. You soon get tired of landscapes. A boy down the road had pictures of musical-comedy actresses, showing their legs. Golly!

Mrs Rideout ignored her daughter's complaint, as Lettice knew she would. Young ladies played the pianoforte. *All* young ladies. And that was that. Lettice sighed and said, 'Shall I attend to the bovos, Mama?'

'Yes, Lettice. But do not take too long. And wear your coat and overshoes.'

'Yes, Mama.'

'And do not let the lantern flare so that it blackens the glass.'

'No, Mama.'

Gratefully and gladly, she donned her outdoor clothes, lit the lantern, adjusted its wick, and went out of the back door to the bovos. Their shed made a bold, dark shape against the night sky: a shape repeated all down the road. Behind every house there was a bovo shed.

The door of the shed grated open on the cobbles and the bovos clumped their feet and grunted in welcome. The lantern's yellow light was reflected back, redly, by their eyes. There were twelve of them, the usual number. Lettice spoke the traditional greeting: 'Bless the animals that bless us!' They grunted back.

Lettice smiled. She walked down the central aisle of the shed, enjoying seeing what the light of the lantern revealed: the simple stalls, mere dividing rails on posts – for bovos were always docile; the heavy, round, friendly backsides, covered with the thick, short, woolly fur – you could twine your fingers into its warm, springy depths; the great, blunt heads, straining round on the short necks to look at her. Cow-like hooves clattered on the cobbles in mild excitement at her presence. Cow-like eyes gazed mildly and contentedly at her. But of course, bovos were not really like cows at all.

'What would I do without you!' Lettice murmured, as she patted the big round rumps. She entered the stall of one of her favourites, Rosie. Rosie made way for her and lifted her clumsy head to be stroked.

'And what would *we* do without you?' said Lettice, to herself. The light of her lantern came from bovo oil. The gas light in the house came largely from bovo excrement. Her shoes were made of bovo leather, her coat contained bovo wool, the meat she ate –

She shuddered and switched off her thoughts. 'Fancy *eating* you!' she murmured to Rosie. 'How *can* people do it?' She pursed her lips primly, congratulating herself on being a vegetarian. Eating poor darling bovos! How disgusting! Yet everyone did it. And no one thought about it.

'*I* think about you all the time,' Lettice told Rosie, quite truthfully. Other people didn't. Lucas didn't even bother to give the correct greeting when he entered the bovo shed. He just muttered, 'BTBTBU' instead of 'Bless the beasts that bless us.' It was dreadful, the way people took bovos for granted.

Outside in the road, she heard the rumbling wheels of a cart. Probably the oilman. He sold candles, lamp oil, nightlights, lubricating oil, polishing leathers. 'All from bovos,' Lettice thought. Bovos pulled his cart – he said they were steadier than horses. Bovos gave the oil that lit the cart's flaring lamps. Bovos gave the hides that covered the cart. Why weren't people grateful? BTBTBU, indeed!

Something rubbed at Lettice's ankles. Catchmouse. She put the lantern down and picked up the cat. 'Your catfood comes from bovos, Catchy!' she told the cat. She put the cat's nose against her own. 'Aren't you ashamed to eat it?' Catchmouse did not answer. She was cross. She wanted food, or attention, or to get back into the house – something of that sort. 'You sulky, greedy, fat old thing!' she said. 'I wish I had your life! No chores, no piano lessons, no school! Why won't you talk to me?'

But the cat's head and eyes were straining from side to side, looking for mice. 'How nice to be a cat,' Lettice said. 'Mice everywhere! Poor little things.' Even as she spoke, Catchmouse clawed and scrambled, trying to escape her. She had heard a rustling in the straw over there: she wanted to get at the mice that caused the rustle. A world that kept and fed bovos was overrun with mice. Every house had at least one cat and every cat had unlimited mice to hunt.

Catchmouse got free and ran to the straw. There were squeaks and scuffles, then a little scream that made Lettice feel sick. Why was the world so cruel? Poor little mice! And Duff chasing rats, trying to kill them. He dreamed of rats, Lettice knew. He told her so.

'You never harm anyone, do you, Rosie?' she said to the bovo. Rosie clumsily tried to lick the hand that stroked her. 'You'd never harm anyone, would you? I wonder what you think about, Rosie. Do you get bored, just being useful and good? Don't you ever wish . . . Oh, I don't know. Why won't you talk to me, Rosie?' Lettice crouched down in the corner of the stall, her eyes level with the bovo's eyes. That was how you made cats and dogs talk to you. And horses and cows. 'Talk to me,' she whispered.

But Rosie only stared back, dimly, lovingly, stupidly. Bovos never talked.

Lettice's knees and thighs began to ache. She stood up, sighed, took the lantern and walked between the double line of bovos, patting each one, and calling it by name.

At the door, she took the halter of the latest addition to the herd – Rosie's seventh son, Septimus. She led the calf, already almost as big as a cow, to the floor troughs at the end of the shed. Septimus had to be toilet-trained. 'Go on, Septimus,' she said. 'Do your duty. Clever boy.'

Septimus swung his head uncertainly, but eventually obeyed. Then, without further guidance from Lettice, he began to amble back to his stall. 'Come back, you bad boy!' she said. Uncertainly, he turned. 'Pull the chain, Septimus,' she said. 'That's right! A good hard pull!' The animal obeyed, tugging solemnly with his big wet mouth. 'He's learning fast,' Lettice thought. 'We take them for granted. We call them stupid. You're not stupid, are you, Septimus? You're a clever boy! You're learning to pull the chain!' He looked at her with his great mild eyes. There was no expression in them.

She sighed and prepared to leave. She called out, 'Bless the beasts that bless us,' then closed the door. At once the warm, mystical smell of the beasts was gone and the night air struck chill at her. 'Cold common sense,' she murmured.

It was a favourite phrase of her father's – perhaps because he showed so little common sense himself. He would never make a mark, never succeed, never win his own wife's approval. Did it matter? Perhaps not. The Lord would provide, the Lord and the bovos. No family could starve or even face discomfort provided that the bovo shed was kept filled with healthy, obedient animals.

'I won't succeed either,' Lettice decided. 'Why should I? I'll just be kind to the animals and try to make them talk to me. *Really* talk to me.'

She shivered in the darkness yet delayed returning to the warmth of the house. Mama would say, 'Why were you so long, Lettice?' and Lucas would say, 'Been talking to the animals again, Lettice?' or something like that. But she *did* speak to the animals, she was sure she did.

Or did she dream it? She had such strange dreams, sometimes. Dreams of another place, a place with lots of machines ... metal machines that ran on fat wheels, going very fast; machines that talked to you, or that you talked at; machines everywhere, all so smart and clever, machines that did everything. There were no bovos in this dream world. Perhaps the machines took the place of bovos?

She shivered, entered the house, put her overshoes on the rack and her coat on its peg and went into the living-room. Her mother said, 'Why were you so long, Lettice?' and Lucas looked up, his eyes alive with malice, and said, 'Had a good chat?' This remark made Papa lower his paper to look at her and everyone started on her, as they always did.

Septimus

In the shed, the bovos talked.

Rosie said, 'She is good and kind. And she likes me best.'

Hector grumbled, 'Fools! You females are all fools! But I . . . I have plans, great plans, wonderful plans!'

The male who came second to Hector said, 'Hector and his plans!' and snorted loudly.

Septimus, Rosie's calf, took no notice of the words of the old ones. He blinked his eyes to make himself concentrate, lowered his head and pushed. The stout wooden boards forming the wall of the shed creaked.

He pushed.

A particular board bulged.

He pushed.

The board split. The jagged edge raised splinters that hurt his nose.

He ignored the pain and pushed.

The splintered board gave way and suddenly something strange and wonderful rushed into his nostrils – cold, clean, night air, scented with grass and trees and starry skies.

Septimus filled his great lungs with the magical stuff – it made his brain spin and glitter – and pushed.

Stubbornly, unhurriedly, he pushed and pushed until at last there was a big, jagged hole facing him. The others pretended not to know or hear; for they were old and stolid, perhaps afraid. Septimus was young. He walked through the hole in the wall. Young, free and angry.

He lumbered quietly down the road till the sheds and houses were left behind him. Now there were hedges and fields, glowing grey and silver and blue in the moonlight; and smells – such smells! – that led him on and on until the hedges were gone too and the neat fields, and there was only IT, the boundless world showing no signs of Man. There were grass and thistles, a scurrying rabbit, a big mushroom palely glaring in pearly grass. And always, the smells, the smells! that led him on.

Nostrils wide, his steaming back dewed, he journeyed on. Clouds in the sky parted and suddenly there was a thing up there, bright and blazing; a round thing, frilled with luminous-edged clouds. Septimus stopped, raised his great head and stared at the moon. It offended him. It stared at him. He thrust his head at it and blew loudly through his nostrils, challenging the moon to come down and fight. But the moon was afraid, it stayed up there in the sky, staring and staring. Septimus shook his head sideways to show his contempt. The clouds closed over the moon and the cowardly enemy was gone. Septimus had vanquished it.

He decided to journey on. He had to pull his front hooves out of the ground. His great weight had sunk them. He heard the sucking noises as he pulled himself clear, and snorted again. 'Big!' he thought. 'I am big!' And now, as he walked, he swung his head deliberately, blowing through his nostrils. When he breathed out, there was a spray of liquid and a fine, loud noise. When he breathed in, there was the smell – a new smell: the smell of his new self, himself washed by the dew, purified by the boundless air, strengthened by every movement of his great muscles. A fine, new, acrid, warlike smell . . .

He began to run, hugely and clumsily, tossing his head,

snorting, thundering. The pounding of his heart made drumbeats and the roaring of his breath was power and glory.

And there was the moon again, broken free from the clouds, the great luminous eye staring at him! Septimus reared on his hind legs – flailed his hooves – and tried to butt the moon.

Septimus was not the only one to escape. Other bovos broke out and wandered into the wilds, seeking other places, other times and tracks.

Nearly all were recaptured and returned to their proper lives in the bovo sheds.

Nearly all, but not all.

Other Puffins by Nicholas Fisk

Heard about the Puffin Club?

... it's a way of finding out more about Puffin books and authors, of winning prizes (in competitions), sharing jokes, a secret code, and perhaps seeing your name in print! When you join you get a copy of our magazine, *Puffin Post*, sent to you four times a year, a badge and a membership book.

For details of subscription and an application form, send a stamped addressed envelope to:

The Puffin Club Dept A
Penguin Books Limited
Bath Road
Harmondsworth
Middlesex UB7 ODA.

and if you live in Australia, please write to:

The Australian Puffin Club
Penguin Books Australia Limited
P.O. Box 257
Ringwood
Victoria 3134